THIS
PLACE
I CALL
HOME

THIS PLACE I CALL HOME

STORIES BY
MEG VANDERMERWE

Publication © Modjaji Books 2010
Text © Meg Vandermerwe 2010

First published in 2010 by Modjaji Books CC
P O Box 385, Athlone, 7760, South Africa
modjaji.books@gmail.com
http://modjaji.book.co.za

ISBN 978-1-920397-02-9

Editor: Priscilla Hall
Book design: Natascha Mostert
Cover design: Jacqui Stecher
Cover artwork: Diane Swartzberg

Printed and bound by Mega Digital, Cape Town
Set in Palatino 10.5/13.5 pt

For my mother,
for always making a house a home

For Grace Paley (1922–2007),
for showing me the way back

Acknowledgements

Thank you Colleen Higgs for your vision; Priscilla Hall for being the most gifted editor a writer could hope for; Arja Salafranca for your helpful advice; Cindiswa Ndlela and Nomakuna Tyami for your Zulu and Xhosa translations; and my friends and family for your endless support.

CONTENTS

A HIJACK STORY

Is one of them coming? He knows this can't be right. He's fled guns before. Held up not to the back of his neck – his occipital crest, under siege right now – but his heart, his very soul.

Uganda. 1972, Idi Amin and his gang of barbaric murders: those bastards came in their jeeps and kicked down doors. Stole your home, your land, assaulted and insulted you. He survived that. So this shouldn't be happening to him again. Not now, not at his age.

The ground is too hot. After a long morning of ferocious Durban summer sun, it's scalding his soft right cheek, the fleshy palms of his hands spread out flat in front of him on the tarmac as the black bastards try to figure out how to override the Mercedes safety lock. His chunky gold wedding ring is already gone – its absence a gnawing worry, like that anxiety when you've forgotten to do something very important. In one of those bastard's pockets. There's a red-skimmed welt in its place where they tore it off. That's not all. His Rolex watch bought in Singapore when he went there for Jasminda's wedding; his wallet; his shoes; his belt that they've used to bind his feet, too bloody tight – it's cutting off his circulation, his feet have already gone numb. First the left then the right, there's a combination of tingling and pain moving in waves up and down his shins. Medically speaking, of course, he knows the pain is just an illusion. Block the body's ability to transmit the neurological signals, the brain's ability to receive them, and the pain disappears, that's how painkillers work. Panado, aspirin, Myprodol, those are the best. The biggest brands aren't always the best but in this case he would recommend it every time unless the patient is pregnant or has allergies. Now so many people claim to have them, you have to be careful, don't want to be sued.

Boom boom boom. His heart is beating too fast, 130, 140, something like that, cantering. God, if a patient came into the clinic with a heart rate like this he'd have to say, my friend you must calm yourself this instant or you're liable to drop dead right here in my office. Pumping pounding. It's become a song in his ears, angry frenzied rhythm of darkest savage Africa, those African drums the savages used to bang in those American comedy films he saw as a boy.

Going to Africa! How everyone laughed. Yes, his friends at Delhi University, they thought he was crazy, but they were wrong; in Africa he's become a successful man. Not once – twice: once in Uganda until Amin, once again here in South Africa. People here are lazy, blacks like these three boys, that's why they never make anything of themselves, that's why they'd never amount to anything and why they have to smash and grab from people like him.

He'll not be afraid of death. If necessary he can break death down to its chemical components, strip it of its pomp down to its proverbial underthings, death thin and pale, chicken wing limbs lying on his examination couch. He's seen it a thousand times, felt the cancerous bulge, dealt the blow as kindly as he could in giving the diagnosis. Sometimes death's won but sometimes he has. Maybe then this is death's revenge. These three boys can't be much more than fifteen, with their modest heights, their slender builds, though it's hard to tell, what with the malnutrition in the townships. The sun, the sweat, how much longer? One is coming. This is degrading. He knows he's perspiring. At first when they first pushed him down here, gun lodged into the back of his head, he thought shit, bloody hell, I've pissed in my pants like a real geriatric. What would his patients think if they saw him like this, lying like this, their doctor in his own filth, how could they ever trust him again? But no, it can't be urine, it's only sweat that's running down his legs, if it were urine he'd smell it – urea, unmistakable.

Suddenly anger, a burning, righteous anger like a muscle seizure. Enough already! They must have had him down here for more than four or five minutes, there are patients waiting for him, sick people waiting for him to help them – Mr Jivani, prostate cancer; Mrs Patalia, diabetes; one patient who comes every Friday to get her prescription, Mrs Nirmal, she will be worried. Will Aisha be able to find the pills where he puts them aside? What will they think, that he has forgotten them, that he didn't remember to write the prescription, that he didn't remember his appointments, that his mind is going? Sixty-five, it's not that old, not old enough to die, Lord Vishnu, please, not like the Dhadas murdered in their beds.

Maybe they have Aids or HIV. Maybe the car, the jewellery, the money will go towards paying school fees and not be squandered in the shebeen or on tik. No, he's a bloody fool, the money *will* be spent in the shebeen, pissed against the wall. Never should have let them in to clean

11

the office, that's probably how they discovered when he left home on Fridays, or maybe they're fearless opportunists, not afraid of robbery in broad daylight. But when he was a boy you worked for it, didn't steal it from others, damn it, that's always been the difference between the Indians and the blacks, this country, whole continent's going down the tubes. Should have listened to Ama, should have sold up long ago and gone back to Delhi like the Goldsteins sold up and moved to Israel. She will insist now, insist insist with tears – but what would his patients have done without him, and what would he be without them? No, he was not ready to retire, sit around all day in Delhi, a foreign place really, after all this time, drinking mango lassi. And then what with the rest of the day?

Voices getting nearer, louder. Are they arguing? Just the tip of one white takkie, about size nine, a few centimetres from his nose. Cheap white, a black cheat, God his heart, in spasm now, he can hardly breathe so maybe he'll be sick. What else will he tell the police? Over their faces, masks. The size of one foot is exactly the size of from here to here from the wrist to the elbow. Is that true Grandpa? Spit has crusted on the corner of his mouth. Sandy grit and burning tarmac on his cheek, the smell of the road. His mouth is completely dry. If he tries to turn his head to scream will the boy shoot and if he shoots and plants the bullet in his brain instant death a severing of the right and left lobes the bone will explode and if he misses and hits the spine he will be paralysed though he'd still bleed to death right here outside his own house left for his wife to find him corpuscles and haemoglobin spilling out of him a leaking sinking ship a battleship there's a hole in my bucket delilah delilah a hole in my bucket delilah a

THE LEOPARD HUNTER

Viktor Gerhardt splashes his face with warm water from the washbasin and, standing up straight, with the soap now gone from his eyes, examines his reflection in the small, round shaving mirror. Yes, he likes it, this new beard of his. It glows dully, with all the humble honesty, Viktor feels, of wood curlings on a carpenter's workshop floor. Never before, during his previous city life, would he have one. A moustache for many years, yes, but a beard! Too, what's the right word?, crude; yes, he considered it somehow crude and a little untidy. But now he wants to look like the other men out here do, these honest men of the land, with their sunburnt skins and beards, like his farm manager Piet Koos and the rest he sees in town, buying life's simple necessities: sugar, salt, cooking oil, feed for their hungry Karoo sheep. More like them and less like his old self. That man is gone – dead and buried the day Adolph Eichmann set in motion the crushing wheel that would eventually make him and those like him at the university redundant.

Redundant. English, from the Latin *redundare*, to surge. What's surging? thinks Viktor. Mediocrity, ideology, hate? Viktor looks down into the bowl of soapy water. He is shortsighted without his spectacles and so has to stare hard to see it clearly, the pale brown dust scum forming on its surface. This dust scum will be left even after the water is tipped out onto the parched vegetable garden and will have to wiped out by one of the native farm girls when she comes to clean his room. Crawls into everything, this African dust, Viktor has observed these past few months – pockets, shirt collars, ears – infiltrating everywhere, silently covering everything, just the scene he'd tried to get away from. And his colleagues at the university? Paul, his old friend and Dean of Humanities, he certainly made his allegiances plain. What's become of him now, Viktor often wonders during the hopeless, bitter moments. Probably crowned Herr Chancellor for his efforts, couldn't implement soon enough. Bastard, standing up, shutting his office door so that his secretary couldn't overhear their last, sensitive conversation.

'Yes, Viktor, I agree. Scandalous. Terrible mediaeval prejudice.'

Voice suddenly sinking low, eyes darting to the door. Was someone listening? Spies already gliding down university corridors and across marble foyers, eavesdropping at keyholes, ready to report back to the Gestapo now entrenched at Hotel Vienna, eating sachertorte. No, he wouldn't help, would only preserve his own neck, the scum. That morning Viktor had watched as Herr Direktor Professor Paul got up from behind his desk and opened the door for all to hear, so that there could be no doubt where his loyalties really lay, speaking his lines as on a stage: 'But my hands are tied, orders are orders. Early retirement, Viktor, accept early retirement or forfeit your pension. No more room for English literature, you must understand, the language of Britain and the Americans. Since our Anschluss it's all about the Fatherland now, the mother tongue again.

We have the future of the new Austria to safeguard and, of course, the future of its students.'

A mask-like smile that made Viktor cringe, an empty handshake and '*Heil* Hitler!' with the right arm shooting up like a military checkpoint pole in the direction of Viktor's back as he strode off in disgust to collect his briefcase, his raincoat and the letter that had arrived that morning informing him of his sudden but immediate dismissal.

He did not pack much that afternoon. His heart and ego smarted too acutely. Had he not, after all, known Paul, what, seventeen years last October, when he was still a doctoral student? Had he and Gertrude not attended the baptism of Paul and his wife Franka's daughters? All forgotten. No, he had made it plain, he wouldn't help.

After their meeting, Viktor had sat in his chair by the window. He didn't know where to start. So many papers, so many books, how to pack up a life in one afternoon? In the end he gave up trying, sat back down at the window, looked out at the treetops. They were in May bloom, buds bobbing merrily on a mild spring breeze like tiny sailors' buoys. The universe lived on, oblivious.

He went home soon after, ate no supper, went to bed before the children returned from school. He'd planned to return to the university the next day for his things, but there was no next day. The following morning they came and ransacked the place, and not only his; the offices of Kohn and Juber in Mathematics, Levi in History, all their files, papers and books tipped into smoking pyres.

And now, to see him here, the once celebrated literature professor, on a sheep farm in Africa, looking like this. Viktor puts on his spectacles and steps back so that he can catch something of his upper torso in the small, round mirror – a farmer in a faded khaki shirt, a rough-necked, bearded peasant. What they would say? What, no more starched collars? No more shiny shoes smelling of leather cream? No more beautiful but naïve doting Aryan students, sighing with admiration as he attempts to seduce them with a Shakespearian sonnet? And he has lost weight, is even going a little grey. And now all the terrible troubles of a leopard on the farm. Such a pity, we hope he wriggles like a worm – that's what they would think, what they would want, the wheeling Fascist vultures. But they're wrong, couldn't be more wrong. This wild country is finally making a man of him, that's right, a man.

Viktor takes off his spectacles, rinses again and gropes for the towel hanging at the side of the washbasin. Pats his skin and beard dry. Puts his spectacles back on. Throws the towel on the bed. Picks up his jacket, his rifle, his heavy ammunition belt, and lifting back the flap of the netting he's had put in as a sort of curtain, steps out on to the stoep into the chattering twilight, soon to be stars in blackness overhead.

The sheep, that's what matters, Viktor tells himself every day, day after day. The sheep, just the sheep, safe for the moment, safe tonight, guarded over there beyond the barn by native boys with rifles – an order given by Piet at his insistence. He can understand their reluctance, why they quivered when he gave the order, their brown eyes wide with fear: the leopard beast that has been terrorising the farm these past five months has shown itself capable of anything. Three native shepherds mauled as they tried each time to fight or scare it off, one fatally. And what is it?, twenty-three precious sheep already gone, more than one a week. But when he finds it tonight, when he does, he has made an oath with himself, and with the farm workers too, that the leopard shall never have the opportunity to kill again.

'Adam, *kom.*' A black man, slim and tall, a rifle slung over his muscular shoulder too, steps out from where he has been waiting for Viktor at the edge of the wooden stoep. The two men set off across the lawn, once green, Viktor imagines, once surely some shade of green, but for so long bleached to parchment by the sun and its terrible thirst that it has forgotten its original colour. It's getting dark and Viktor wants to be high on the koppie, above the dam, by nightfall.

The two men walk quickly and in silence together towards the fence that separates the farm from the vast plain of scrub grassland and thorn bushes. Viktor has decided that he will take the lead initially. He knows the way from here until the dry riverbed and the foot of the koppie, but after that, Adam will have show him where to go, how to track it, because it's true, he doesn't yet know this terrain as well as Hans did, and probably never will. His brother Hans, he hears from Piet and his Boer neighbours, liked to walk out into the open veld at night without another living soul, liked to sleep like a native, without a canvas tent, on an unrolled mattress, beside a campfire. Probably too drunk to pitch a tent, Viktor thinks, as he climbs over the fence, his boots landing with a solid crunch on the dry bush.

And *what* of Hans? The two had hardly spoken by letter these past years before Hans's death. Then this was all meant to be his brother's good joke, wasn't it? – leaving the city professor a sheep farm about to go belly up, a hundred thousand miles from... what can he call it?, can't call it home, not any longer. Hans would have laughed at the whole damn lot of it: Hitler, from petty beer house thug, to emperor; the very real anschluss; the very real behaviour of the university and his fellow Austrians. Yes, even at his elder brother and his sister-in-law's serious predicament – all of it, Viktor thinks, as he walks. Hans always saw the serious as no more than a joke. Still, the particular joke of this mess of a farm, broods Viktor, this particular needle against his elder and only brother, whom he knew never thought much of rural life… 'It might just save our lives,' Viktor says to himself softly, so that Adam walking a few paces behind cannot hear. Mine, Gertrude's, the children's, Mama's. 'And give us somewhere safe to flee to' – that is, if he can save this bloody mess of a farm first.

Time is running out. If they are to have the best chance of catching this leopard unawares and killing it, then he and Adam must reach the lookout spot before the sun, already red and low, has completely melted down beyond the ridge. Viktor squeezes the rifle a little closer to his chest. There is sparse yellow grass or even thorn bush for Adam and him to hide in here. The long drought has taken its share; the grazing sheep and veld fires the rest. But up there on the rocky escarpment of the koppie, where he has been told that creatures like this leopard like to lie in the shade surveying the plain and farms below, there are good places to watch and wait for it to make its way down in the moonlight to the dam to drink.

No sign of the leopard yet, though? No tracks, Adam? No spoors?

'*Niks?*'

No, Adam shakes his head, nothing yet. Yes, they must wait. Viktor screws up his eyes to look at the dark silhouettes of the thorn trees in the near distance. He cannot believe it: bare, not a single weaverbird roosting on a branch, no sign of any other creature for that matter. Probably all at the dam, now that the sun is almost down, all looking for water. There has not been decent rain in this area, Viktor has heard, for nearly three years. The watering holes and streams for the animals have dried up, all but the dam, and on the farm the reserve boreholes will soon be dry too. New ones must be dug, Piet says, if the sheep are to survive until next market. That will begin, the search for good water, when Piet returns from Springbok with his mother-in-law in one week's time.

Yes, the struggle to survive will continue, Viktor knows, even once this damn leopard is shot; it's naïve to think otherwise. But this leopard – and this is what he could not tell Gertrude in his last letter to her, knowing how she would react, knowing what she would say, but he has convinced himself – if he can just kill this leopard, then the rest will somehow fall into place. As he walks now, rifle in hand, he has this feeling – Gertrude would call it superstition – with only more certainty: find it, kill it, this one enemy; succeed with that and somehow the farm, finding water, and all the other challenges – Gertrude and the children, his mother, their permissions, the money to bring them here, the sponsorship and all the rest – it will all be easier, more possible somehow. But no, he didn't dare tell Gertrude this, only addressed the concerns that she said were most pressing: what to do with his books, those that had not yet been confiscated – sell them, give them away, now that once again they are being forced to move.

What would she say about the kill? He knows already. 'You are losing your mind, playing cowboys out there in

Africa. Crazy talk, superstitious like a negro savage. It is not logical, Viktor, do you hear me? Totally illogical.'

But it's all illogical, isn't it, dearest Gertrude, Viktor concludes, a taste of bitterness, like chicory coffee, filling his mouth. The world has been turned on its head, where good people are forced to leave their homes, forced to give up their possessions, their jobs; wear a badge; take a beating; hand over pets. For God's sake, every week another illogical edict, all without rationale, except to inflict another more deadly wound. Obey! Forbidden on Pain of Death! No Jews to Keep Pets! – the edict published in the newspapers and on street corners three months before he left. Their cat, Lady of Shallot, who every evening, as he Viktor sat at the fireplace in the apartment, a plate of Clara's sweetmeats at hand to stave off pre-bed hunger pangs, mewed at his feet relentless until he slipped it something delicious and then let it jump up and curl into a luxurious purring ball on his lap. That cat gone, like his job; taken by Clara and given to her parents. They needed a good mouser, Clara said; better that than dead, Gertrude told him.

'But it is our damn cat!'

'Shh, not so loud, Viktor, she might hear. And the children, Viktor, think of the children, you know how upset they are.' And the Levines from the apartment across the landing asking, 'Can the edicts become any more preposterous?' Meanwhile the tears as Mrs Gunter led her pet daschund down the steps into the streets, its small body bouncing happily, sniffing the flagstones; going walkies, it thought, not knowing the truth, that it was on its way to the vet to be put down because she could not bear to give it away to complete strangers. After Viktor saw that, he had closed the curtains in the sitting room with a sharp snap and refused to go down into the streets for three whole weeks, lest he laid eyes on one of their damn flags. And meanwhile. What, the rest of the rational, logical, reasonable world looks on and does nothing? Be reasonable, says Chamberlain, Hitler is not being *unreasonable*. 'There thou mightst behold the great image of authority: a dog's obeyed in office' – that was King Lear speaking. Viktor shakes his head, his whole body threatens to tremble with rage, like a plucked string. To hell with that logic, with that *reason*.

Up ahead, about fifty yards, the dry red river bed. He can just about make it out in the deepening dusk; and just beyond that, the foot of the koppie. When darkness comes to these parts, it comes almost absolutely. Soon there will be no light but the scattered light of the stars and then later the waxy wash of the full moon. The veld, it is a place at its most magical at night, he has heard, but also at its most dangerous. Already his muscles feel more tense. He holds his rifle tighter, his finger ready around the trigger. He feels naturally more alert. This is the hunter's instinct, he's been told. But animals like this leopard, they have the advantage over humans: they can see you, hear you, smell everything. Still, this thin breeze, it's in their favour, blowing towards them, cooling their nervous sweat, carrying their scent away from where the leopard probably is and where it might be able to sniff their approach. Isn't that how it works?

Hans, what would he say, looking down with the distant stars on his brother who mourns the loss of a spoilt pet cat, yet now hunts? Who hunts, yet as child could not stand the sight of a drop of blood; who, when Hans fell from the slate roof of their childhood home into the cobbled courtyard below and bled from a wound on his left knee so profusely it created a dark puddle that the doctor slipped on, hid in their father's study amongst the calm columns of leather-

and cloth-bound books until it had all been washed away and Hans was bandaged and safely tucked up in bed.

This is what life has done, dear brother. The last two years, terror, bitter humiliations, and the sense, sometimes unbearable but always present since the invasion, of impending dread and doom. The sense that time is running short.

It came to him, this leopard; came to him in a dream three nights ago. Already he had made up his mind that he could wait no longer to hunt it down and kill it. Piet was away but another sheep had been lost that very morning and he had told himself, no, no more. When the moon was full, as he knew it would be in four days' time, tonight, and so giving the best light on the nocturnal plain and dam, he would go with Adam and find it, kill it. Time was running out.

And then that very night the leopard came to him. He had passed several hours tossing and turning in bed, unable to fall asleep, his mind filled by the stifling heat, not a breath of air, and jangling with the words of Gertrude's last letter, the children, the university, Paul, problems of the farm, the lost sheep and how to find the money needed alongside the stock losses, how to untangle the bureaucrats' nets to get the family out. Then, just as he was falling asleep, finally sinking beneath that black blanket like a man going down into a mine, something happened. He felt it for the first time, near, very close and getting only closer. Suddenly, no longer was it swallowed up and hidden by the night as it prowled around the farm workers' tin and mud huts, no longer looking for sheep to pick off as the rest grazed near the dam in the daytime but actually inside the main house with him, beside his bed. He couldn't believe it. Its warm, low shadow, and still smelling faintly of sweet, sticky sheep's blood, the animal it had caught that morning beside the dam and gorged itself on. Grumble in the pit of its throat, then seven short coughs. He began to sweat, his heart pounding. Get up, he told himself, get up and shoot it, for God's sake. But he could not, his body would not, could not move. Walking now in the pale moonlight at the foot of the koppie, Viktor clenches and unclenches his right hand around the barrel of the gun. It was as if these very muscles were paralysed that night in the house, petrified, like the creature Adam showed him last month when they were looking for a missing sheep, down in the ravine where the ancient river used to flow and gather in great crystal pools, a prehistoric fish, preserved for all eternity in a block of stone. And then, just when he thought that it would leap on him, kill him, tear him to pieces as he lay helpless, it was gone. No, it seemed to say, not tonight. and padded out of the house into the noisy African night.

Yes, time is running out, he feels that too. So tonight he cannot fail, though he knows he isn't a crack shot, though he knows he has done something almost impulsive, almost as foolish as Hans might have done, coming out here tonight without Piet, without another white man, only Adam. A Karoo Boer like Piet, he has heard, though he has yet to see it for himself, can shoot down a row of copper pennies, one after the other, lined up neatly on their sides on the fence at forty paces. But he can shoot, yes. Has learnt these past five months, and is determined to learn after tonight, after this leopard, his first, how to do it well, as well as any other man can. There is only one worry – that when he is actually confronted by the beast he will falter, as he did in the dream. That worries him a little: whether the thought of extinguishing a life, something alive, to take a life, any, that point of energy, of vitality gone from the life force of the universe forever, will somehow cause him to falter. Nothing else. He is not afraid; no, is no longer afraid for himself.

When did he know? When did he realise that all was over, that all was lost? He has asked himself that question many times over these past months. It was that day, walking home from the shoemaker, clutching his brown parcel tied with string, about three months after losing his job, that he saw them, the sweets in the shop window of Schumacher's on Florenstrasse, each tin, each individual sweet, emblazoned with the black insignia of the Fascists, an insignia which he remembers from when he first saw it on a pamphlet, reminding him so much of wheeling carrion vultures. He came home and told Gertrude, 'They are feeding it to their children. There is a queue out of the shop and into the street.' Two fashionable girls sucking on them, schoolboys squabbling over their share, parents carrying the tins home, wrapped, he told his wife, as gifts. Finished, all gone. All over. It will not end now, he told Gertrude, until it is too late. For months, since the blow at the university, he had been going around in a blurred, wounded stupor; his pride, his ego. He had even been holding up a vague hope that he would be reinstated in his old position. But now he knew. 'We must leave here, Gertrude. Must find a way to get out. Anything.'

But all avenues tried brought nothing; the embassies in chaos, the Jewish organisations helpless. Panic, rats leaping, tails thrashing, trying to escape a burning ship. He was nearing his wits' end and suddenly it came, a *deus ex machina*: a letter, something positive, if you could call it that, from an H Hani in Vrosburg, a place that at the time he Viktor could not even imagine, but it sounded to him, ironically, almost German. A Vrosburg attorney, executor to his brother Hans's estate. His brother dead, circumstances unclear but basically a heart attack, the doctor said. And he, Viktor, heir to his bachelor brother's sheep farm in the semi-desert South African Karoo: seventy hectares and five hundred head of sheep, though drought was wiping them out fast, the letter warned.

He could have guessed her reaction when he told her his plan, to come out here, salvage what he could and then send for them. But why South Africa? Why not America, England? Try the embassies again, she pleaded try the universities again; write another letter to Charles Felton in Manchester. Anywhere but that farm – think of the children. She grew weepy, flushed in the face. He too, as their voices raised, and the children sitting up in bed, listening to their parents' row. He imagines them now, that night, Maria with her hands over her ears, Yanis sucking the corner of his sheet, as he has done since he was a little boy.

'Do you think I want to go and watch sheep? They do not want us here! This is our chance, maybe our last and only chance, Gertrude.'

God. What *will* Gertrude say when they finally get here, when she sees this wild and barren land? How will she *cope* out here? She will have to, as he is learning to, to train his mind, to turn it and bend it, to accept what he cannot understand or explain; to learn about it, when his whole adult life has been about teaching others. Now everything must be explained to him by Piet, with all the patience of one trying to impart knowledge to a thick-skulled child or one of his most mediocre students, from how a sheep is birthed to the chemistry of chemicals that are used to dip them; from the parasites they catch from grazing in one spot too long to how a sick animals will always break off from the rest; and how water for a new borehole can be found by a talented man clutching a forked stick and feeling the tremors of the deepest earth through it. Good God, at the end of the day as he tosses and turns sweating in his bed, his mind reels like a spinning magic lantern. Sometimes everything seems to be no more than chaos. And now, these past five months, more so with the arrival of the leopard. But for the moment, still no sign of it, just the smell of the African dust, Viktor thinks, as he creeps forwards, crouched at the foot of the koppie, the heat of the day finally fading off the scorched land, evaporating as quickly as water. As children, he and Hans used to go with their father, walking up in the mountains every summer in the Tyrol, he and Papa collecting flower samples for Papa's experiments, later to be logged in the journal, dissected, sketched, whilst Hans ran ahead, screeched from cliff faces, shot at butterflies and birds with his catapult – a laugh, always looking for a good joke.

'Up here, Adam? Continue up into the koppie here?' Adam is nodding as he moves carefully forwards, and yes, he can see the dam clearly already, just on the other side of the cliff face, like a sheet of metal, or polished glass reflecting the silvery moonlight and the dark silhouettes of animals' bodies as they come to it, bending their necks and heads low to drink or wade slowly in, to wallow in the cooling mud. Any moment, he is sure. He can sense it. Any moment.

Of course he and Papa never hunted. Not killers; civilised men, they thought, men of books of a civilised country. The better sort. 'Baas...' Stop. Adam is holding up his hand. He has found a crevice, a crevice with a clear view of the dam, where they are to crouch and wait. His fingers to his lips.

Shh. Crouch low again. Not a sound, could be deadly any moment, Viktor knows this. His heart is pounding fast now, fast and hard, as it was in his dream, only this time it will be different; this time he will kill it. It is coming, moving slowly down the stone hillside, leaping from rock to rock, slinking down between the crevices, subtle and smart as a shadow. He can feel it. Yes, all that matters is here and now. This leopard. This act. This moment. Time is running out, he feels that too. He must kill this leopard, must kill it tonight.

HOTTENTOT VENUS GIRL

Hendrik my freed kaffir boy and I were stumbling along. Money was tight, you see, getting desperate and I without prospects since falling out of favour with my superior, General Grey. I had set our sights, Hendrik's and mine, on pastures new, the lucrative trade in exotic live curios that was all the rage back home in England. But what to sell? Everyone there thought they had seen it all. Leaping lions from blackest Congo and treacherous tigers from Bengal, grrrrrr. Pot-bellied pygmies from Southeast Asia, and Siamese twins all the way from that country. I had to decide fast, make my move, as it would soon be a case of the poorhouse or no house at all, not only for myself, still a bachelor, but also for dear, loyal Hendrik too, and his wife Anna and their little boy and girl, if my assets as their Master continued to liquidate at the alarming rate they were doing.

I had an idea. Something spectacular. Something with...

'What, Master?' Hendrik asked, picking ostrich meat from between his ivory teeth as he and I rode together in my carriage through the Company Gardens.

'Something.' I spoke my thoughts out loud as had become my custom with Hendrik, 'Something,' pondered I. 'I will know for certain once I have seen it,' I told him and drove the carriage on, past the Magistrate's Court, towards the dark heart of the liberated slaves' quarter and Hendrik's lodgings.

She was in the sunlight outside Hendrik's cottage kitchen, shaking a blanket free of straw and mud. She was standing in profile, dressed in her snug servant's smock. For some time, years, she had performed as nursemaid and cook in the Hendrik household since she and her tribe were seized in the valley of the Gamtoos, but so far her other qualities had, shall we say, been overlooked. I could see it, well, everyone, even a dimwit could see it, there was no denying it, her extraordinarily large, er, potential. Unable to contain my excitement I stepped down from the carriage and hurried inside with Hendrik. Before the fire she now stood, stirring a pot of soup on the hearth. She was just as I had thought. Quite astounding, a perfect specimen. I held my kerchief to my nose to temper the choking fug of smoke and curing buck hides. I peered closer through the thick air in that little room. Yes yes, a body like Eve, swung down from the trees, brown as river mud, round as... It was round. Erect, and erecting, one might say.

So I whispered in my manservant's ear, 'Hendrik, see there, our fortune is guaranteed by that very derrière. *Gluteus maximus.* Her lovely face too. People back home think they have seen it all, but they have never seen a backside like that, my dear boy, of that I can assure you. What a rump! We could sell her by the pound. Rumptuous! We shall call her our Saartjie, our Hottentot Venus.'

29

We tied her up, but not with ropes and chains. With pretty promises. With sparkling dreams. We drafted a contract, a binding legal document for six years, an all-expenses-paid holiday, we told her, to the great and civilised lands, with pearls in your pockets, diamonds around your neck; and then, if you so desire it, a ticket back to the land of your birth. How about it?

We grabbed her and wrangled the necessary paperwork. I pushed some favours with dignitaries, Lord Caledon among them, whom I had once cured of the clap. It was no simple smuggle. She was precious cargo but also a tempting titbit for our fellow travelers, who immediately wanted their cut. The merchant sailors in Saldanha where we boarded (she, Hendrik and I) wolf whistled and ground their groins; the toothy one-eyed skipper cocked a smile and leaning closer demanded, 'How much for one night to bed that dark sow?'

'No no,' cried I, 'Her dignity please, and room to breathe. And must you all crowd round? And if you must, can you not do so later, in London, where for a mere two shillings each, a most pitiful price, you too shall have your pleasure?'

Three months the ocean voyage took from the Cape of Good Hope to Southampton, and no easy journey it was. Our treasure spent much of the time on deck looking southwards. No promises of fame or fortune on my part could soothe her as she wept for the land she missed and believed she would never see again.

'Come come, now now. Why all the fuss, my dear Saartjie? Have I not given you my word, as an English gentleman? Do not fear. Now let's see that routine again, the one where you shake and shimmy in your ostrich feathers and sing your pretty tune. The curtains please, Hendrik.'

A physician by training, I had been forced by enemies most foul to magic myself into the role of theatrical impresario. Yet I think I showed a natural flair for it and so, in the end, the last laugh was mine. Once at home in London, she was, as I had predicted, an instant and most triumphant success. Size is what matters in the smart city sets, you see. On the opening night, women of society and men of wealth all swooned at her feet, fans flapping, lorgnettes squeezed in sweating palms, in the packed display room of Number 225, Piccadilly, across the street from the infamous Liverpool Museum. By the end of our first week, she cleared the bill. There was no competition. Next door, the freak boys of Farnham closed without so much as a wheeze; across the street, Rubber Chan sat on his hands; and every fashionable drawing room from Mayfair to Brentwood spoke of nothing else but this Hottentot Venus, this tantalising savage temptress who had crossed oceans to be explored and shared by the citizens of London town, but whose stay in the metropolis would be brief.

In short, the good people flocked. Paupers, princes – there were queues around the block. But ignore the filthy rumours; I impress on you, I never abused her, I merely used her for the betterment of us all. With success assured she was treated like gold, put on a pedestal – a 7-foot-high stage, to be exact, where she emerged from her hay hut sucking on a clay pipe beneath the flickering oil lamps. A silk body covering left something to the imagination, but not too much. 'Make sure they can see her *areaolae erectae*,' I had whispered into the ear of the blushing Chinese seamstress who conceived the costume on the block in Limehouse.

I am not one for life on the margins. She lived the high life of London, complete with. horse-drawn carriages and creamy champagnes. Every tear she shed, I insist, I mopped up personally. Wrung out into little glass vials, those saltwater drops sold for a shilling a bottle. And for a guinea a quart, the milk in which she had bathed in the silver tub at the mansion house of the charming fourth Duke of Queensbury, who described her later, in a letter to royalty, 'as the most delicious crouton ever to land in the soup.'

She was adored by artists, and preserved in their various capacities by scientists, the greatest zoologists and physiologists and anatomists of the day on both sides of the Channel. One French scientist fellow, Cuvier, as I recall, came along and wanted her coaxed from her shell so that he could carve her out, naked. He erected his easel. He eyed her and sketched her but it itched him that she would not allow him closer, to examine her pubenda in all their exquisite detail. He was a perfectionist. Who could fault him? But it was no simple cajolery, that I can tell you. That girl, when she so desired, could be as slippery as the greasy banks of the Egyptian Nile, as stubborn as the most bull-headed elephant.

'Now now, don't play so coy, Saartjie. We know how you dark lot really are. Be a good hottie and drop your hide apron so that these fine gentlemen can see your –.'

Considering all, she made out rather well, simple country girl that she was, one born without the means to realise the vistas of promise that her natural endowments offered. Some do say that she was lonely, but I never saw it. Hundreds came to see her every week, thousands over the years, and I think she was grateful for the attentions after a youth spent in oblivion with only the wild animals and her father's cattle for company. And there was always Hendrik and myself. We never left her side. She was free to be with us, day or night, for a sympathetic shoulder to cry on, a warm body should she need warming in the cooler climates. And when I could no longer be with her, when I grew sick and lay on my deathbed with life's twilight drawing close, I left her in Hendrik's charge. 'Be a good boy and take care of her, Hendrik. Be a good boy, won't you?' But there was something about his face that I did not recognise. A paleness to his complexion, a sly greedy glint in his eyes.

I hear, echoing through to my present state, that she never did reach home again alive, and that the fortunes too somehow passed her by. But know how we loved her. We loved her, all of us, and none more than I. At times, I confess, it was a sacrifice to share her with the others, and when I finally expired it was her name that lingered last on my lips. As she slipped permanently from my view and beyond my reach, I sighed my death sigh: 'Oh hottie, sweet sweet hottie, our Hottentot Venus girl.'

THE HOLIDAY

Martha Samuels is house-proud. It pains her to see that overnight, whilst she was out working the late cleaning shift at the offices of Du Preez, Sons & Associates in the Mother City – vacuuming passages, tipping out waste paper baskets, scrubbing the stains from their communal coffee pots – someone has again dumped junk on her front doorstep.

This time, *wat nog*? An old grey child's takkie, just one with no laces, a car radio, its wires hanging out like worms, and two Brown Ale bottles, all left right on her doorstep for her to clean up. *Yessus*. She pushes at the takkie with the tip of her shoe. Useless. The radio also, it has taken a beating. What, someone try to steal it, Martha asks herself, try to steal it and make a mistake? She drops them both in the rubbish pail ready for next week's collection lorry that may or may not come. But the smashed bottles, those need to be swept up.

Martha will not have her house, or even the street that surrounds it, look deurmekaar. Even at sixty-five. Even with her son and his five children to look after and her energy quietly leaking away from her daily, as though from a slowly dripping tap. Inside, you could eat off the wallpaper, the second-hand 1950s wooden sideboard, the faded linoleum kitchen floor. Five decades of keeping house for white people, she knows what is necessary to clean this mess up. Martha bends down and squirts Handy Andy into the stainless steel bucket that she has filled with boiling water from the kettle and carried outside. The raw, toxic smell of the detergent rises up with a cloud of steam as she swings the water across the pavement with an expert gesture, then begins to sweep. Five Roses Tea later, milk and sugar, four spoons. Mmmm, Martha thinks, that'll be something lekker. And after? And after, there will be supper to make. When her son gets home he will be hungry. He and his children eat and eat. Mouths fall open faster than she can fill them with curried mince and rice. White bread spread thick with real butter. Growing strong, that's good. Strong enough to get the bloody hell out of here. Maybe go to another city, any, open your own business, man. Here is no good, Andre, she tells him every day when he comes back complaining with the same story, that no one wants to give a man like him a job.

'Ma, something for whites, now something for the blacks, but for us coloureds, even if you've got the qualifications, nothing. *Fok.*'

Yessus, Martha thinks as she sweeps, that boy always has some or other excuse. But it is true what he says, for us coloureds it's only getting worse. Just last Sunday after church, when she and the other women on the church committee were standing together drinking coffee and eating koeksisters, Irene told her another horror story. About a neighbour walking home from the bus stop. It was not late, but she was tired after all day ironing at the drycleaners where she works. Her eyes were on her aching feet and she walked down Mopanie Street just thinking of getting home to take her cool bath and fry the packet of chicken thighs she had bought. A clapped-out Toyota Corolla pulls up, out jump five coloured boys, 'could have been our own grandsons they were so young,' all with the same red t-shirts on – 'means they belong to the Good Life gang.' Before this old woman could shout or make a scene or do anything, they pushed their pistols at her as though they'll shoot without hesitation. 'Hey Ouma, bang bang bang.' They stole her purse, even her bag of shopping, then roared away, the wheels of their motor spinning on the asphalt, their laughter dirtying the twilight air like rubbish stink.

'Did she go to the police?' Martha asked.

'Agh,' Irene shrugged wearily, 'What's even the point? What will those blerry skollies say? We know it's because the gangs are bribing them that they do nothing for honest people like us. And soon this area will be just as bad as Mandalay. Just as bad.' Martha leans on her broom and remembers Irene's look of pain as she muttered, 'At least under the Nats we didn't have to worry about all this crime.'

Martha is going away. Taking a holiday, a real holiday away from Mitchell's Plain, this city, this country with all of its mess and problems, away for the first time in her sixty-five years. She has already booked and paid for her ticket. She can hardly believe it.

And Andre? The rest of the family? No, they were not pleased for her when she told them. 'What about us?' her granddaughter Lela asked, pulling the stereo headphones from her ears. The twins just looked. No. Martha shook her head. 'Me alone.' Her son Andre sat back in his chair and stared at her darkly over his bottle of beer. For two whole days he would not speak to her. Then he said, 'How long you been planning this behind our backs, hey?' He wants her to feel guilty, she knows, for spending the money on herself. For secretly scrimping for the past forty years, five rand, ten rand, three rand, one rand, fifty cents, for the past forty years, and then not only not telling him or anybody else about it now that he was one year out of work, but throwing it all away on herself. 'And on a *holiday*? Have you gone completely *crazy*, woman? What does someone like you know about overseas? You're just a coloured who's never been further than Bloemfontein.' He laughed bitterly and took another swig of beer. When he said that, Martha had pushed herself up from the table. She was angry, yes, but no, she did not say anything. Just did what she always does when her son gets drunk and says things that offend her, that is, cross to the sink, turn on the taps and, jerking up her sleeves, put her hands down deep into the greasy mouths of pots and pans and in a furious silence begin to scrub and scrub and scrub.

Martha picks up the bucket. It is too hot for sweeping. Sun is beating down on tin roofs and sweating heads, making sweeping too hard work, making her tired, giving her a hell of a headache under her doek. But in France now, in Paris, she knows it is winter. The air is fresh and clean. And snow? Martha inhales and then exhales slowly. When she leaves in a month's time, that travel agent Susanne has promised her that there will be snow.

She wants a Panado and her cup of tea. Martha bends down and, picking up the broom and steel bucket, carries them inside the house. She has left the lace curtains in the tiny living room and kitchen drawn. Everything is quiet. No noise of bickering grandsons and granddaughters or the blerry television. The usually crowded rooms are empty. Their leather and denim jackets are not cluttering up the sofa. It is lovely. She carries the bucket to the sink, fills it with warm water from the tap, then sets it down on the floor. Before she leaves to go to work she must remember to wash out the bath and bleach the toilet. Also put the potatoes ready to roast in the oven. Martha picks up the kettle, fills it, listening to its rumble, then returns it to its place on the hob and turns on the stove. The blue gas flame quivers under the kettle's aluminum base. The kettle begins to whine gently. She opens the cupboard above the sink and takes down the white pill container. With difficulty she twists off the top and shakes out a pill. Too large to swallow down on its own and it will be bitter. She squeezes her tongue against the roof of her mouth in anticipation and fills a teacup with tap water. She will eat a rusk after.

'I just don't understand you, Ma. How long you been planning it behind our backs? How long?' Andre asked again, standing over her at the table this morning. Martha holds the pill to her lips. How could she tell him the truth about what happened more than forty years ago?

Martha thought she had heard every story there was to hear about white madams from her ma and her ma's sisters when she was a girl growing up. By the time she was fifteen and ready to leave for the city to begin full-time domestic work herself, these were some of the stories Martha had heard. About madams who locked all their cupboards so that you had to ask permission to get the sugar for their coffee, or another bar of carbolic soap – these madams spied on you because they thought you would steal but they turned a blind eye when their male visitors crept into the kitchen to pat your buttocks. About madams who did nothing when their children were rude to you. Who bullied and who bossed. Who, after three years of loyal service, dropped you without decent references because they claimed you were clumsy and had secretly chipped an expensive teapot or a favourite china vase.

Of course there were good stories too, not all the tales Martha's ma brought home twice a year to her nine sons and daughters up in Kamieskroon were bad ones, but Martha's ma and aunties all agreed that a maid and madam, they can never be friends. And that's what Martha herself had always believed, until she met Miesies Claire.

The first time Martha met Miesies Claire it was in Miesies Claire's front garden on a spring afternoon. Martha remembers stepping past the open wrought-iron gate and seeing the madam of the house standing alone on the front lawn. It was late, past lunchtime in the suburbs. The southeasterly was blowing and the temperature was not so warm, so why is this white woman still wearing nothing but her pink silk sleeping slip, Martha thought as she approached Miesies Claire across the grass. At first glance she reminded Martha of that white film star Elizabeth Taylor at the Metro bioscope. She was young and small, *pragtig* and a real figure. Also she had coal black hair cut in a bob that blew in her face in the wind. It was only when Martha got close that Martha saw that she had been crying – her eyes were swollen and her cheeks bright pink like someone had given them a good hiding. God, Martha thought. But it was too late to turn around and go. This white madam was expecting her.

'I've come about the job, Madam. You need a domestic?'

Miesies Claire turned and looked at Martha. Yes, Martha was sure now, *sy het gehuil.*

'What's your name?'

'Martha, Madam.'

In silence Martha followed, down a long, wide, cream-coloured passage, past the dining room with it mahogany dining table and walnut sideboard, and into the kitchen. The whole house smelt sharp from fresh paint, and in the rooms with their doors ajar Martha glimpsed all the chaos of cardboard boxes that were only half unpacked.

Standing with Martha in the kitchen, Miesies Claire didn't look at her references. She shook her head and waved the letter away. 'I've got myself into a mess, Martha. You see, I've got people coming for dinner tonight and nothing's ready. Can you cook?'

Martha nodded, 'Yes, Madam, I can cook.'

'Then you've got the job.'

'Thank you, Madam.'

'Only...' Miesies Claire was taking in Martha's appearance. Martha could feel her running her eyes from Martha's slender face to the worn-out shoes, the single suitcase she had not yet put down. 'Please, don't call me Madam. Makes me feel *so old*. It's Mrs. Claire, and Mr Claire when the bastard's here, which he never is at the moment.'

So that was it, Martha thought, the reason for the fat tears. Martha had never before heard of a white madam who spoke in such an honest way to a coloured servant. Usually they speak to you either strictly, or as though you are simple and never went past Standard Two in school. They never take you for an equal and so when Miesies Claire addressed Martha like so, making it plain from Go that in this house there was between master and madam, problems, Martha took it as a hopeful a sign that this

Miesies Claire would be a different white madam from her first one, Miesies Oliver.

Miesies Oliver. Sies. Standing in the kitchen with her new madam, it hurt Martha deeply, remembering what that great cow had done to her. To show such a disregard for Martha's right name, like it was what?, like the name of a dog. When Miesies Oliver discovered that she and her new maid shared the same first name, she had wrinkled up her pug nose and proclaimed: '*O nee, ons kan nie dieselfde naam hê nie.* Oh no, we cannot share the same name. Not the madam and the maid. I'll call you Josie instead.'

Josie? Two years Martha had worked like that. Scrubbing laundry, bleaching their stink toilets. But after that she could tolerate the name Josie no longer.

Miesies Claire showed Martha the fridge. It was packed full of food, only the very best meat and vegetables, 'Are these all right?' her new Miesies asked. 'I hope so. I'm expecting six for dinner tonight. My mother-in-law, a total dragon, and the rest of my husband's family. Could bore you to tears, all of them, but this is my first meal for them since we moved here from Jo'burg and I want everything to be perfect.' Miesies Claire took Martha to the dining room sideboard where the china was kept, also the silver, and said, 'Can you make a soup and roast? Also vegetables, whatever you want, only my mother-in-law won't eat carrots. And a pudding for dessert? I need it done by seven.'

Miesies Claire left Martha alone in the kitchen. Martha would not see her again all afternoon. Martha put her suitcase down, took off her coat, hung it on the back of a chair and set to work. Four hours the preparation took. She was lucky that she was born a naturally skilled cook and that her aunties taught her so much. Martha chopped and pounded and stirred until everything was in its place, *reg*. She made a roast beef, rare in the middle but with the edges well cooked, to suit everybody's taste. Cream of tomato soup, four veggies including roast potatoes and boiled peas, and a chocolate mousse flavoured with brandy from a half-empty bottle she had found at the back of the kitchen cupboard. It was hard work, but by the end it looked and tasted good. Martha was pleased. When the Miesies saw it she was pleased too. What would she have done, Misses Claire said, if Martha had not come along? Miesies Claire admitted, 'I'm a dreadful cook, can't even brew a cup of tea, I'm ashamed to say.' But there was no time for talking. 'The guests will be arriving any minute,' said Miesies Claire. By this time the Miesies had changed into a long red dress. It hugged her round backside and mango-sized breasts. And she had painted her lips and rouged her cheeks and made up her eyes.

Miesies Claire touched her hair; felt its shape and asked, 'How do I look Martha? And my hair? All right?'

Martha definitely didn't know what to say to that. Normally a white madam never asks such questions. Before Martha could decide how to answer, the doorbell blared through the house and Miesies Claire hurried off to welcome her guests.

That night everyone cleaned their plates. There was not a scrap left for wrapping up with clingfilm and putting in the fridge. Listening at the kitchen door, Martha heard the Miesies's mother-in-law praise her food. 'Your new coloured girl ... a decent cook.'

'Her name is Martha, Miriam. Seventeen but a magician. Came today like an angel and I don't think I could ever survive again without her.'

Martha blushed. A mistress who noticed, who defended her name and who praised. Ja, she had definitely never known a white madam like this one before. She felt that inner warmth, that pride. With her hands she smoothed down the new white apron that Miesies Claire had found in one of the boxes and given her. Uniform spotless, house spotless, everything beautiful in this big house. Yes, she felt that all was good, that perhaps this would be a decent job.

After only a few days Martha learnt the rhythms and rules of the house and her new unusual mistress. Martha had the house to herself each morning – Miesies Claire would sleep until about ten. At that time, Martha would take her in a cup of white tea and a slice of brown toast spread with butter and honey. Miesies Claire did not like to be woken suddenly, so Martha would enter the master bedroom without a sound, the breakfast tray balanced so that nothing spilt. She would say, 'Good morning, Miesies', then slide the tray onto a low table beside the bed. Tiptoeing to the window, she pulled back the curtains to let the sunlight fall in. In the bed the Miesies would stir from her dreams, stretching and yawning like a lazy cat.

After breakfast in bed, Miesies bathed, then dressed. Martha helped with this too – finding those clothes that Miesies Claire couldn't, fetching the towel, running the bath and pouring in one tablespoon of lavender bath salts. The evenings were much the same. Misses Claire went to bed at around midnight. At about eight Martha would bring her dinner, sometimes in the separate dining room or on the back stoep if the weather was pleasant, but usually in the sitting room on a tray, where the madam of the house, Martha soon understood, passed most of the day waiting beside the big black telephone. Before bed, Martha helped the mistress to undress. Hung up her clothes for her and made sure everything was put away in the right place. Miesies Claire said, 'I'm so forgetful. I always seem to lose one shoe of a pair. It doesn't help that I'm a bit of a piggy.'

There was no denying that Miesies Claire was spoilt, yes. Really, the madam was, Martha imagined, only three or four years older than she was herself, but she reminded Martha of a child. But during those early weeks, Miesies Claire treated Martha better than any madam Martha had ever heard about. Miesies Claire was never rude or bossy. She wasn't the sort of madam to stand over you and make you feel your work was inadequate. She never interfered with Martha's cooking or criticised her cleaning. No, the madam had no interest in how her house was run so long as everything looked good and meals were on time. And she was appreciative and even at times affectionate. Daily she poured out her gratitude:

'Martha, I don't know how I ever got on without you.'

'Martha, you are the *most divine* cook. I could eat seven portions of this soup if it wasn't for my hips.'

'Martha, you have a gift. Everything looks so orderly, so neat and tidy after you've been in a room.'

'Martha, won't you help me, you know I can't manage any more on my own without you.'

Talking to her friends who worked in neighbouring houses, Martha was reminded of how things could sometimes be and how at her new job her circumstances had improved. She just listened to Linda complain about her madam's endless fussing; or to Claris saying how her madam's old Alsatian had kakked and pissed all over the blerry place with Claris left to *maak skoon*. 'And those children, they just walk that dog's kak right through all the rooms. Are they totally blind or do they just do it to give me some extra work on my knees? *My Vader!*'

Martha had to tolerate no such insults. 'I think I've been lucky this time,' she told her friends after she had been with Miesies Claire for about a month.

'Lucky?' Claris, who was five years older than Martha, with two children back home with her grandmother, needing food, and pencils and books for school, all of these worries on her mind every morning when she woke up or as she lay alone in bed at night, waiting for sleep, snorted. 'Yes, sure you're lucky!'

'Shshh. No, I'm serious, man. I hardly see her. She spends all day in the sitting room just waiting for her husband to call.'

'Why? What's the matter with her? Is she fat and ugly?' Claris laughed. 'Probably he found better white tit now.'

'Sies, Linda, why you always talk so filthy? Claris, tell her to wash her mouth out with soap.' Martha's friends winked at each other, but Martha ignored them. 'Miesies Claire says it's because of business. But it isn't right. She's young, they've only been married one year. She doesn't even have any children. They've just moved here but all the time she's talking she wants to go away, poor woman.'

'Poor woman? Who spends her life lying around? God. Be serious man, Martha.' Martha did not listen to her friends. A white woman could be like Miesies Olivier, but she *did* feel sorry for this one, Miesies Claire. Money wasn't everything. And she looked *stok alleen*. In her first few weeks in the house Martha had noticed that apart from herself Miesies Claire saw almost no one. Once every second week her husband's family came to the house for a meal. They never came to visit otherwise, and she only went to visit them if she had to. Besides that, Miesies Claire never left the house except to have her hair done at the beauty parlour or do a bit of shopping. No other white madams or friends ever came to the house.

Maybe if Miesies Claire had children, Martha thought, life would be better for her. She would have the babies and their needs to keep her occupied. Her new mistress seemed to spend every day just waiting for her husband to return. And when not waiting for him to come, she was waiting for his short telephone calls long distance from Johannesburg or for a letter. Like a lonely, young and beautiful queen she waited beside the telephone in the sitting room, re-reading gossip or fashion magazines or listening to Cliff Richard records.

Miesies Claire never said when her husband was actually expected home and Martha realised that this was because she herself did not know. Who was this Mr Claire, Martha wondered, and would he ever come back? Martha was not so sure she herself even wanted him to return. How would things be in the house with him there? A man such as this? Nee, it could never be good, only bad.

How long? How long had Martha been working in that house, when Miesies Claire first began confiding in her? A month, maybe even less. One afternoon, Martha remembers, she was dusting and polishing in the sitting room when suddenly Miesies dropped the magazine she was reading and declared, 'The real problem is, Martha, I'm so bloody lonely here.' She said it like a woman who was fed-up angry, but there were tears too beginning to shine in Miesies Claire's big brown eyes. She often cried, Martha knew, in the privacy of the sitting room when Martha was busy doing other things. Martha stopped wiping and lowered her yellow dust cloth and her bottle of polish. After a long pause, Miesies Claire spoke again. 'Sit down, won't you, Martha, please?'

Martha obeyed. She sat down awkwardly, as far away from the madam as she thought would be expected, on an armchair opposite Miesies on the sofa. Martha was still clutching her dust rag and polish. She was careful not to put them down. She waited for Miesies Claire to speak, not knowing what to expect next.

'Thing is, Martha,' Miesies Claire sighed, not looking at Martha, blinking back tears as she looked out of the patio door, beyond the gentle blue of the swimming pool, beyond the lawn beginning to go green with spring, at the neighbour's high wall, 'What if it isn't a factory keeping him away from me?' She turned back to the coffee table, picked up her cup, stirred it calmly before taking a sip. Martha was careful to keep her eyes down on her lap. The mistress's voice sank to a hoarse whisper. Martha could feel she was leaning closer now: 'I mean, what if it's another woman?' Martha listened. The sofa creaked as Miesies Claire leant back again and sipped her tea. Then she put the cup back on the tray. Martha noticed how the Miesies's small hands had begun to tremble.

Martha could not believe what this white woman was confiding in her. She shifted awkwardly on the edge of her armchair.

'I'm ashamed,' admitted Miesies Claire. She knew how the others in Cape Town must judge her. One year married and already her husband was off, doing who knows what with who knows who. Who? Who? She listed the names of women in Jo'burg that Martha had never seen, and talked of which of these was guilty of betrayal.

'And what have I done wrong?' Miesies Claire moaned. She was a good wife, attentive to her husband's needs and she knew she was an attractive woman. Very attractive. She had been Varsity queen and men still turned to look at her in the street. Miesies Claire faltered mid-sentence and Martha wondered if she was crying again but did not want to look up to find out.

'I need a break from all of this, Martha. That's what I need. A holiday from all of this.' She gestured to the house, their surroundings, 'It feels like prison.'

The two women sat in silence. After a few moments Miesies picked up the plate of biscuits that Martha had baked for her that morning and, leaning across the coffee table, she offered one to Martha. Martha hesitated. She took one, but didn't eat it. Still Martha didn't know where to put her eyes. Why was this madam breaking all the rules by talking to her like this? Why offer her a biscuit from the same plate? Martha did not know if she liked it. It was too much. What would come of it? She slipped the biscuit into her apron pocket for eating later and kept her eyes fixed on the white girl's carefree smile on the magazine on the coffee table. When Miesies Claire spoke again she sounded better, even relieved. 'Thank you for listening to me, Martha. It's good to know I have someone I can talk to, someone I can trust.' Martha stood up. She tried to nod and return Miesies Claire's smile, but she could not.

After that first afternoon, two, maybe three weeks passed before Miesies Claire again asked Martha to join her. Once again Miesies spoke about her husband and Martha listened. And after that second afternoon together, the Miesies began to ask Martha to sit with her every day after lunch.

Slowly Martha learnt to forget her fears. For some reason this white woman trust her, Martha realised. She was not treating her like a coloured, not even like a maid, but like a *woman* – a woman in whom Miesies Claire as another woman could confide about her *mal* man and her troubles. What she needed was a patient ear who, as Miesies Claire herself said, would not judge her badly. Every day, excepting Martha's days off, Miesies Claire spoke, Martha listened. And one rainy afternoon, Martha in expressionless silence watched as Miesies Claire twirled in front of the bedroom mirror, laughing in her ivory wedding gown, then suddenly stopped, sank onto the enormous double bed, and wept with all the bitterness of a lady who had just found her husband under its sheets with another woman.

After those tears on the dress, Martha would have liked to have told the mistress, 'Ja, just forget the bastard. He's no good for you. Leave. Go some place else. You'd be better off free.' But Martha knew: Listen, but keep quiet, that's the rule. Perhaps, Martha thought, if she did actually answer one of this woman's questions about what she should do, then there would be problems. And Martha liked this job. That is, she preferred it to her previous job. So, yes, she held her tongue, bit her lip. And prayed each Sunday, when the priest asked, 'Is there any one you should be thinking of?', that Miesies Claire would realise her stupidity in waiting for a man such as the one that smiled so handsomely but so distantly from the silver frames that Martha polished on the mistress's bedside table every afternoon.

Martha had been working for Miesies Claire for three months when one morning the large parcel arrived in the post from the travel agents on Adderley Street. Martha was called into the sitting room. Entering, she caught a glimpse of what her mistress was reading. Not her usual fashion magazines, but what looked like a book of photographs. Well-dressed whites sitting at sunny outdoor cafés. Unfamiliar buildings. The rest of the brochures were piled on the coffee table, all with *American Express Travel Agency, Cape Town* printed in bold gold letters in the top right-hand corners.

Immediately Martha sensed that the Miesies's mood was different, improved. 'Look at these,' Miesies said excitedly. She held one out to Martha, 'Sit down sit down, have a look.' The Miesies began to giggle. Martha was confused. What had happened? She sat down and waited for Miesies Claire to tell her.

'I've made a decision,' Miesies Claire announced. 'I'm not going to wait around any longer. I'm taking a holiday. A grand tour of Europe to blow some of the bastard's money. I only need to choose where. Can you believe it?'

Martha said nothing. She rested the feather duster across her lap and gingerly accepted the brochure that Miesies Claire offered her.

Miesies was still talking. 'When I'm away the bastard can stew. You can't just treat a new bride like this. What do you think, Martha?'

Martha smiled but she was not listening. She was looking at the bright colour pictures in these wonderful magazines that Mr Claire's poor, foolish wife had got herself. Martha had never seen buildings as beautiful as these. 'Paris, France, the City of Romance' the top of one of the pages said. Grey and so distinguished. Arches. Carefully, slowly Martha turned the pages. Immediately she loved the arches, especially the very large one, with what looked like Jesus Christ himself, riding in a golden carriage on top. Her eyes drank in those faraway places. Martha didn't know why, but paging through that brochure and glimpsing the photos she got a deep sense of pleasure. Reluctantly she lent across the coffee table and gave the brochure back.

'Oh, Paris. Yes, Martha, a good idea. Paris we *have* to see. David and I never made it there on our honeymoon. He took me to Venice, but not Paris.'

Martha blinked. She looked at her madam, 'Me too, Madam?'

'Oh yes, Martha, of course. I can't go on my own. You'll have to come with me, if that's all right. I can't possibly manage without you.'

Martha was stunned. Was this a joke? But Miesies Claire was not smiling, she was not even looking at Martha but folding down the corners of pages in the magazine that Martha had just admired. Martha's eyes went down to her feather duster. There were ugly pieces of lint caught in the black feathers. Could this really be happening? Was this white woman really going to take her to those places overseas?

Martha thought to herself, it is not yet lunchtime but what have I already done for her today? Before she was even awake? All the silver, including all the cutlery tipped out onto newspaper on the kitchen slab and polished with

Silvo using an old toothbrush and buffed with a soft rag before being slipped back into their velvet pouches. All the cushions taken outside and beaten together to bang out the dust. Before she was even awake, I moved the sofa she is now sitting on and swept behind and under it. Carried the heavy carpet outside and shook it. Polished all the mirrors with vinegar until they sparkled. I aired the beds, even those that have not yet been slept in. I swept the back stoep. And this afternoon, when she goes to have her hair done, I will cook her fish and soup.

Martha is a practical woman. She accepts hard work. And she believes that Jesus Christ gives us our just rewards. Maybe all her honesty, all her hard work – maybe she had earned this?

That afternoon, when Miesies Claire went out to her hair appointment and Martha had the house to herself, Martha decided she would go back to the brochures – just one more look, just in case it really was true. But first she went to the kitchen and took from the tray the cup that Miesies Claire herself had used that morning. Miesies Claire's red lipstick marks were still on it. Martha put the cup in the sink – she would wash it in a minute, but first she took another teacup out of the cupboard for herself. Then she took the milk from the fridge and filled the cup almost half. This was how she liked it. She went back to the sitting room, the tea balanced expertly on a tray, and sat down on the sofa to read the brochures properly. Old, noble buildings and shops filled with expensive dresses and souvenirs for those with the money to spare. Canals. Hotels like kings' palaces. No-tre-dame. Did it have something to do with a woman? When she came to the photographs of Winter Paris, those beautiful buildings and churches capped in flakes of white, she stopped. She had never seen snow before. It took her breath away. Martha exhaled. *Pragtig.*

That night, lying alone in her bed in her outside room, Martha struggled with herself. For the first time in Martha's seventeen years she allowed herself the luxury of daydreams. She wondered what would it be like to be in one of those photographs. To live one of those photographs. Was she really going to visit those beautiful places overseas? To drink a cup of delicious coffee in one of those pretty French cafés? Stay in one of *those* hotels? See real snow and that building that they called the Eiffel Tower? Why not? Why not her too? Thank you, Jesus. Martha got out of bed and knelt beside the bed on the hard concrete floor. 'Baie dankie for Miesies Claire.'

What's the first thing Martha did? Saved some of her wages. Stopped going to dances and to bioscope with Linda and Claris so that she could buy some special things to take with her. A blue dress good enough, she hoped, for the journey. And how could she go with such a beaten up old suitcase? And without gloves or decent shoes, she needed those too. What she couldn't afford to pay for she bought from Pep, that sold clothing to the coloureds. Get it now, that's what that shop used to promise, pay nothing for a whole year. 'You'll need a coat. It's snowing,' Miesies Claire warned. 'The French call it '*nei-ge*.' Martha wondered how she would find the money to pay for a coat too. And at night Martha dreamt of tall buildings piercing the stars, and fields of snow as white and bright as Omo washing powder.

With the promise of their holiday, of their escape, maid and madam were given new energy. Martha worked even harder than before, trying not only to meet all of her mistress's needs but to anticipate them. Miesies Claire seemed more lively too. She rose each morning now, nine o'clock sharp, and with Martha's help unpacked the boxes in her bedroom and in her husband's study that had stood untouched or only half organised for months. Back and forth to the travel agent she went, with a tireless will, and bought new clothes and luggage for their flight.

Martha and Miesies Claire still had their afternoon talks. But now Miesies Claire no longer only spoke of herself or her husband. All conversations revolved around their planned trip: where they would go, what they would visit, what they would eat and do, applying for documents so that Martha could travel overseas. She didn't tell Linda and Claris, she didn't dare. She would go and come back and only then tell them then. They would not be pleased for her. No, they would be jealous. There would be rows, bitterness.

Time passed. November became December. The ocean beyond the Sea Point promenade turned from ash-grey to a sparkling blue. The date for their departure, in the first week of January, was only a month away. Martha woke in her outside room each morning to birdsong everywhere and the sight of the Christmas flowers, blooming balls of pink and lilac on their bushes outside the double garage, and she felt happy for the first time in her life, really happy, a feeling she would not know again until her sons were born.

Still, after all these years, one question: What would have happened if Miesies Claire hadn't received that telephone call? Martha does not know. All she does know is that one week before they were meant to travel, with Martha's suitcase already packed, Miesies Claire was woken by a call from Mr Claire. The problems with the factory in Johannesburg had been resolved, Mr Claire said. He would be home in Cape Town by the end of the week, in time for Christmas.

Time passed quickly after that. The Miesies spent the days getting the house and herself ready, having her hair done, fussing over small details, buying even more new shoes and expensive dresses. It was not long before, for the first time, she stood over Martha inspecting her work. The last of the boxes from the move, why had they not yet been unpacked? Martha would need to do that. And polish the silver, the cutlery too. And freshen up all the rooms and prepare the feast for the party for Mr Claire's return. Did Martha have time to run to the florist? Why had the butcher not delivered? With so much to do, Martha was not invited to sit and speak with Miesies Claire in the afternoons. No more mention was made of the trip to Europe. Would it be delayed? Rearranged? Martha waited each day for Miessies Claire to tell her but each day Miesies Claire said nothing, though her suitcases remained out and ready.

What happened next? Mr Claire came home. That's right, there was the big party and a week of fuss. Martha had to adjust to having the master in the house. He was nothing like she'd imagined all those months. Early to rise, hardly spoke a word to Martha. Short, quiet, *dik*, he and his wife kissing and courting all day, even in front of Martha, without shame, like teenagers. He was, Martha recalls, also very particular about his shirts. Yes, Martha remembers that well; wanted no creases. So what happened? He and his shirts went with the madam on the holiday, the holiday that Miesies Claire had promised her. They went alone. Martha was left behind.

The couple were gone for two months. When they came back Miesies stood in her green travelling coat in the entrance hall and said, 'Oh Martha, it's so good to be home. Everything looks so wonderful,' and turning to Mr Claire as she handed Martha her vanity case to carry upstairs, 'Didn't I tell you, David, that she's a marvel?'

Now, forty years later, standing in her own house, Martha shakes her head. No. That's a lie, what Miesies Claire said. Already her work had deteriorated. There were signs, signals to greet the couple when they returned, though Miesies Claire, Martha remembers, had pretended not to notice. For example, the brass front door knocker, Martha had not polished it in weeks and so it had gone grey and dull. She didn't sweep the stoep or bother to tell the gardener to scoop the leaves from the swimming pool. The returning husband and wife found nothing waiting for them in the fridge. They shuffled as they stood, perplexed and patient, as she emptied a can of Campbell's cream of chicken soup into a pot, then turned up the stove so high that the soup burnt. Though, by nature she is house-proud, cannot stand by long enough to watch dust settle, she was not able to get any pleasure from her tasks and the doing of them as she once had. She no longer cared if Miesies Claire praised her.

Later that evening: 'We want to give you something, Martha.' Out from the luggage came a small plastic globe that swirled with snow and suddenly Paris was a blizzard. 'That's the Eiffel Tower,' Miesies Claire said, 'It's a famous building in Paris.' Martha held the plastic globe. She had never felt so terrible. She put it down on the kitchen countertop beside the dirty soup bowls and went to her room.

Rebellions. Over the coming weeks and months it got worse. She left the capers out of the potato salad. She didn't wait for the hardboiled eggs to cook for a perfect twelve minutes and sometimes fragments of shell, missed by her quick skinning fingers, found their way into their guests' egg sandwiches. Sheets she began to change every other week. Sometimes she left a red sock amongst the white wash and watched as the sheets and underwear, and Mr Claire's shirts, emerged a blushing pink. For a further two months it went on like this. Then she could not stand it any more, she gave her notice. And Miesies Claire? By that time Miesies Claire had looked only relieved to see her go and pay her her last wages.

The kettle is whistling on the hob. Martha steps forward and turns off the gas. She goes into her room off the kitchen and to her chest of drawers in the corner. Her new suitcase is already out at the foot of her bed. What does she still need to buy for her journey? Woollen gloves, a heavy warm winter coat, boots thick and tough enough for snow.

Snow. *Ne-ige*. Martha has been practising the French word for months. *Ne-ige*. She pulls open the top right-hand drawer of the chest and takes it out of its tissue-papered box the Paris souvenir from Miesies and Mr Claire. She has kept it these forty long years so as not to forget but she has never shown it to Andre or anyone else in the family, or told them about Miesies Claire and the promised holiday. Martha looks at the globe. It is small and surprisingly heavy on her open palm. Martha looks and watches and, as she does so, the sleeping snow around the feet of the 2-inch-high Eiffel Tower slowly begins to stir.

EXILE

At the luggage carousel inside the international arrivals terminal, Alan waits in silence with the other passengers, still tired and groggy from their long overnight flight from London. Some chat softly in Afrikaans, their hands in their shorts pockets as they watch and wait, impatient for their bags to come. Alan stands, his legs slightly apart, facing the mouth of the belt. He is waiting for the familiar brown leather suitcase to appear. He imagines dark hands of men in blue airport overalls lifting it off the wagon and dropping it onto the slowly revolving mats. Alan thinks back, sees himself at Heathrow locking the suitcase – a complex and expensive padlock; possessions go missing from bags all the time in Jo'burg's OR Tambo airport, he'd been warned. He sees himself at Heathrow pushing the suitcase on a trolley and placing it on the baggage scales; then the pretty young checking attendant at the Virgin Atlantic counter as she pressed the foot pedal that whisked the bag away with a whirr. He sees himself at home too, the moment when he decided to transfer everything from the suitcase on his bed into the old case from his parents' bedroom cupboard, the case that had to come back with him. All these images seem to occur in Alan's mind in a single instant.

Alan is not his real name. No, his real name is Jongilanga, though he hasn't used that Xhosa name since he was a boy more than forty years ago. As a child in exile in London, he soon learnt that the name Jongilanga made the other English children in the local boys' grammar school laugh and the teachers irritable as they stumbled over its pronunciation during morning registration and in class. Soon his name was shortened to Langa, then somehow these letters were reshuffled like Scrabble tiles and the 'g' dropped, until finally they became Alan. By then it was the beginning of the school's spring term. The family had been in England since October. After a few weeks he took the name home with him and insisted his parents and sister call him by it too.

'That's a stupid name,' his 14-year-old sister had commented over dinner. 'What does it mean? It has no meaning,' she said. Alan had turned to look at his father, watching for some sign in his father's face of disapproval or disappointment. His sister, Celani, also waited. She did not mention that, almost on the first day of the previous term, she allowed herself to be renamed Catherine by the nuns at her convent school, a name she would also soon adopt at home. But nothing, their father had said nothing. No, already by then he was increasingly silent, already a man in exile from himself and from his family.

Alan sat over his food, toying with it with his fork. On the end of it not *mieliepap* (that could not be bought, his mother explained) but rice. So you have forgotten us and left us behind, Alan thought bitterly as he stared down at the tasteless food on his plate. First you bring us here, now you don't even talk any more. I hate you. It had been a turning point, Alan remembers, one of the many in his deteriorating relationship with his father. Meanwhile outside, the cold English rain fell and fell, impatiently drumming on the window glass and gargling along iron gutters and down drains.

A few minutes ago, stepping off the plane, feeling the thick African heat for the first time in more than forty years, Alan remembered. He remembered things he'd thought forgotten or considered so deeply buried that that were as good as permanently forsaken. Not only the memory of that evening with his father over dinner when he tried to shock him with the news of his new name, but before, when they still lived here. Himself still a South African boy lazing in the South African sunshine. His father taking them to see his family on the Wild Coast; the heat of the car even with all the windows rolled down and the thrill in his bare legs from the scorching car leather. Then outside, picnicking in bathing costumes on deserted beaches, his father with his nose in a book' his mother under a bright yellow beach parasol, spreading a lunch of sandwiches, chicken and fresh fruit juices out onto the towels, and himself and his sister barefoot, always barefoot, digging in the white pepper sands.

In England, the young Alan would also learn, the children never walk without shoes, not even in the summer, and the sun never shines with the same primordial intensity as it does beneath the Equator. For their first six months in England he, his mother, his sister and father had sat in the house huddled around the gas fire trying to shake the damp chill from their bones. At meal times they hunched over their food in rollneck woollen jerseys that itched and scratched and seemed like straitjackets. The woollens and waterproofs, the thick tights his mother had bought herself and his sister and him too, were even starker and more painful reminders of their exile for Alan than the unfamiliar surroundings of Alan's dead grandparents' tiny maisonnette in Lewisham and the bitterly cold autumn and winter London weather.

With time Alan grew used to the dark dull days. It's true. He grew used to the grey shapes of English buildings, the supermarkets with expensive fruit and vegetables that tasted of nothing.

But Alan had never got used to his new name. So why had he kept it, clinging to it for all these years? He knew then and he still knows now: to punish his father. Far from home, stuck in a foreign place where his inner longitudes and latitudes no longer met at a familiar central point, where you couldn't even buy a tin of Milo and where the child of African political exiles was a target for curiosity and hostility, Alan had felt doubly betrayed. Back home in Jo'burg, at least his parents had had their circle of friends, politically alive blacks and whites, people who accepted them warmly for who they were. In England they seemed to know no one. No one ever came round late at night to talk. There was no laughter and drinking in the sitting room, no poetry readings by his parents' friends; no talk of who had been followed home, of who'd never arrived home but had simply disappeared on the way back from a party meeting, work, a trip. Alan and his sister used to creep up to the door and listen, standing barefoot in their pyjamas and ready with stories of bellyache and sleeplessness if an adult found them. Sometimes the adults let them stay in the room, up late past their bedtimes, drinking flat Coca-Cola from glass tumblers while the adults drank whisky with soda and read poetry. Sometimes Alan's father read some of his. Alan would watch with pride as his father took his spectacles from his breast pocket, opened them with one hand and put them on. Usually he recited standing up, but occasionally he sat down on the high-backed chair beside the mantelpiece, his typed sheets in his hand or one of the books that had been printed and then smuggled into the country illegally at Alan's father's risk and the risk of the foreign publisher.

Alan's father's poems are sad, angry poems. Alan never realised that before, though he knows some critics have said it. Like that academic in America, at North Carolina, for example, who considers himself such an authority on all of Alan's father's work. During the past few weeks in preparation for this journey and the grand ceremony tomorrow, Alan read them all for the first time in years. Looking at them now as an adult, with his father twenty years dead, he has had to swallow the lump, like a bullet, in his throat. Back then, though, all those years ago, before the family left for London, while still a boy sitting in their house in Soweto township, his father's poems had seemed magical, yes magical, if only half understood. As a boy he comprehended only fragments, a word or a phrase, like a fine stained glass window with only individual panels or colours illuminated. Sometimes, after hearing his father read in his clear, serious voice, Alan would go to bed and lie until he fell asleep with one of his father's metaphors or half-snatched phrases still in his mouth, on his tongue, beautiful and deceptively simple, like smooth beach pebbles.

When exactly did the writing stop? Alan cannot remember. He has been trying to, trying to recall precisely, for weeks now. When they'd arrived in London, he knows, the third bedroom in the house had been reserved as a study. Inside, everything had been arranged exactly as it had been in his father's study in Soweto. And each day during that first difficult autumn and winter, Alan's father had gone to his study as he had before the family went into exile, but there was no sound. No sound of punched typewriter keys. Silence. Nothing.

And then after a few months, or was it weeks, his father stopped even pretending to try. When one day his son asked why he no longer wrote, his father had replied, 'What is there to write about?' He had left it, this, his country, his subject, his home, behind. Then he turned from his young son to the window and once again watched as the drizzle fell outside.

Perhaps that wasn't the end of it, Alan thinks, watching the slow snaking of luggage before him. Perhaps it was the second and final arrest of Bram Fischer that marked the real end of it. When word reached them that Alan's father's friend, the respected Afrikaner lawyer and secret head of the country's Communist Party had been arrested a second time and would almost certainly be sentenced, he had taken the news very badly. They could not have been in England more than a few months. Alan remembers it as he stands now, looking at these jovial whites in shorts. These tourists too, all wanting their piece of the new, free, rainbow nation South Africa.

'Are you visiting for business or pleasure?' the passport officer had asked the woman in the immigration queue beside Alan. 'Oh pleasure. Pleasure, of course,' the elderly English lady beside him had replied with a smile. Do they know, really *know*, Alan cannot help but wonder, wonder with some bitterness (yes) what so many went through, all those dark years ago, to make this a reality? Alan remembers his father's cracked voice. Tears? Was his father crying? They didn't know he was awake, thought he was asleep. He had crept out to the bathroom and heard them.

He imagined his father, a man who before they moved to England had always seemed so invincible to him, as mythical as a giant, on his knees, his head in his wife's lap, and his mother, soft, always soothing, stroking his cropped Afro curls.

'We shouldn't have deserted them, Linda. I have let them down. I've been a coward.'

And his mother: 'Hush, shh. You'll feel better about things in the morning.'

That had been a bitter blow, to hear his father describe himself like that. Was he a coward? As the weeks turned to months, to years, and he watched his father grow more taciturn, more selfishly withdrawn, Alan decided his father *was* a coward. A fucking coward indeed, who abandoned first his country and then his family, when both needed him most.

'But what did he do that was really so terrible?' – the question, Alan recalls, asked by Pamela when they had just begun to date and were exchanging histories and stories about their families. How to try to make her understand, how to explain, to put into words for another, such a private, personal betrayal? She looked at him puzzled as she drank from her glass of white wine and waited.

'He was the heart. The heart. For as long as I can remember, we all moved and breathed by his sound. Then when the heart went silent, the body died. And he allowed that to happen. That was his choice and he allowed it.'

His future wife smiled and nodded, but Alan knew right then and there that he could never make her see.

His own son Patrick, living with his mother up in Scotland, did he judge Alan as harshly as Alan once judged his own father? Rather than trying to work it out with Patrick's mother, he had chosen to throw in the towel. Who knows what Patrick thinks? They barely seem to speak these days since he started university. He wanted Patrick to come on this journey, to make this journey together as father and son. They could be like that man and the teenager standing over there talking about who knows what. How long till the hotel? Where's the luggage? Will they see lions? But together at least.

Yes, he judged his father harshly and continues to do so, just as Patrick judges him. But the truth is rarely so plain, he knows that from his work as a journalist; always two, three, four sides to every story. So what was the truth? What would he say tomorrow night if asked? There have been biographies written, he knows, biographies about his own father by strangers, like that academic at North Carolina, that for years he's refused to participate in or even read. But over the past six months he has picked through them, trying to separate the biographers' truths from his own, to find his father's truth amongst the obsequious verbiage. How bland their family turmoil looks, on paper:

> It was after the poem about the first arrest of Communist Party leader Bram Fischer, when a bomb was found under the family car, that his wife Linda convinced Otha to leave and return to her native England, a country that would provide her and her husband with British passports if he wanted them, and a safe place to go at least for a time, until things cooled down or the government was forced by international pressure and sanctions to see sense.

Does Alan remember this? He remembers the secret conference in the family living room, adults in a state of heightened agitation. Yes. People going to and fro through the house all day, making it seem to him then almost as busy as this airport. The next day at dawn they left. They did not drive in their own car; an associate of Bram Fischer's, temporarily released from police custody after his first arrest, and at great personal risk, had arranged their departure. He and his sister Catherine were not allowed to pack more than a small bag each. Most of their luggage space went to their father and his typewriter, books and papers, the most precious ones being packed into his father's brown leather suitcase.

For Alan, aged ten, the whole two days leading up to their arrival on the Mozambique border had seemed like a tremendous adventure, like something out of a spy novel. Their father had kept them singing songs, the kind they sang when they went to the Wild Coast for family holidays. At the border they had changed cars again and crossed over to Mozambique in the dead of night. It was only when they were safely in Mozambique that his parents allowed the strain to show. Even then, it was only the family who saw. For the biographers, his father had indomitable strength that never wavered, strength that gave strength to others:

> When Nelson Mandela was eventually released from prison after more than a quarter of a century of imprisonment on Robben Island and then Pollsmoor Prison, it was Otha's Mansani's poem *Survivor's Song*, published in 1957, that the President said had helped keep his spirits going and which he would chant in his mind each morning as he completed his ritual of exercises.

Tomorrow will be a new dawn for you,
And then the hills alone will cry tears.

When they first arrived in England, Alan's father would occasionally say that his imprisonment and Nelson Mandela's had begun at almost the same time. Mandela on Robben Island, Alan's father's in Lewisham in London. But whereas Mandela would eventually be released, Alan's father would never see his imprisonment end. He would die nine years before Mandela was set free, sixteen years after first boarding the plane from Nairobi to leave for England with his wife and two young children. A ghost of his former self, he never penned another word.

After her husband's death, Alan's mother had chosen to remain in the house where her children and husband had spent those painful years. Alan does not deny it. He left his mother to care for his father alone as soon as he was old enough to go away to university in Edinburgh. Like his sister Catherine before him, he fled – anything, anything to escape the oppressive silence of his father's typewriter, the deafening quiet in the house.

Recently, when he had decided to get back to South Africa after all those years, he had contacted Catherine in the States. He wanted to talk to her, to invite her to come too.

'Do you ever think we were too hard on him, Cathy?'

'Jesus, Alan, what are you talking about? It was terrible.'

And the ceremony to honour their father in South Africa? 'No. It's all so long ago. I moved on, you know. But you go if you want to.' So there it was: permission.

The years of strain of living with their father had taken their toll on their mother too, once a beautiful woman who loved dancing and company, whom Alan remembers as a child always glistening like a jewel. By the time he left home it was all gone, the bastard had dried her out. And now? Now, twenty years the widow, she rarely goes out unless Alan insists. Alan knows he doesn't see his mother often enough, or Catherine. Last time he saw Catherine in the flesh, it was in Philadelphia just after Patrick's third birthday, fifteen years ago. Maybe when he gets back he will try to sort something out, some sort of family reunion.

Six months ago, when the call came through from their mother about the letter and invitation, it was left to him alone to catch the tube from Canary Wharf after work to go back to the house and discuss it with her. He rarely went to that house any more. Really, he had not been inside for years. Stepping through the door he was surprised to find it all there as he remembered it: the narrow, dark entrance hall with a place for hanging umbrellas and coats; the front room; the pink carpeted stairs; the dark wood furniture left by his grandparents when they died and which made him think of gloomy coffins and grey corpses when first he saw it. And the rest – the typewriter with the blue plastic cover, his father's notebooks with the neat, rushed handwriting that always slanted far to the right, as though his father was in a great hurry to get the poems out before his exile began and the words dried up.

He sat with his mother on the old bed that his father had always kept in his study so that he could nap if writing exhausted him. The cup of tea that his mother had made for Alan grew cold in the cup as he read. There was to be a cultural centre, the Otha Mansani Cultural Centre of Racial Tolerance, opening in Johannesburg. Nelson Mandela would to be present as the opening and he himself was going to recite one of Alan's father's poems, *Freedom Now,* that helped keep the flame of hope alight in his heart through the dark, apartheid years. The ex-president had heard the sad news that Otha Mansani had passed on during his own time in captivity. Would his remaining family, his widow and their children, be willing to honour the people of the new South Africa with their presence at the inauguration?

The letter was signed by the Minister of Arts and Culture. Together they'd examined it beneath the lamp. It looked genuine. What did she want to do? Did she want to go?

No, she wouldn't go. No. She shook her head. But if he wanted to go, he could, and he could take the papers too, and the typewriter if he wished. 'You go,' Alan's mother had said, 'and take your father's things. Maybe they can put them in a museum, in a display case. Your father never would have liked that, of course.'

She went to his father's desk. Alan felt a spasm of pain to see how his mother had left it untouched all these years – notebooks, pens and pencil, Waterman ink bottle, the black ink long ago congealed and dried – everything exactly as he'd remembered it, no doubt as his father had left it. And the typewriter with its blue plastic cover, the ivory-coloured keys just visible. She pulled open the drawer and brought out a bundle of school exercise books, which she put in his hands. These were the kind his father had always used, now discoloured with age.

Then she had gone into her bedroom and come back with the brown leather suitcase. With sudden recall, Alan recognised it as the one his parents had packed that night back in early 1965, when he was ten, the one they packed quickly. And then they all left before sunrise, through a neighbourhood still asleep, for the Mozambique border and so to Nairobi and finally a plane to exile in London.

He has agreed to come, yes, but not for his father. For the ex-president, a man he deeply admires and knows to be old, maybe near the end of his own great journey. Alan watches a black couple, the woman in a dark green silk dress, the man in a beige suit with a gold tie and tie pin. These are South Africa's new black middle class. Some of them will celebrate his father's poetry now, the sort who would want to use his name for a school or a hospital. You may be a hero to them, father, but don't think it's just like that for me. I'm not so sure, father, that I can forgive and forget so easily.

Alan picks the suitcase off the caravel and slides it gently onto a trolley. For the last few weeks he's been seeing so much of the past. It's true, the past is everywhere. But suddenly he sees the future. At customs he will hand in his green declaration card and push the trolley to the exit. Outside there will be crowds of faces, white, black, brown, all waiting together, their faces expectant but all strangers to Alan. Some will have flowers, others balloons. As he negotiates his trolley through the people he will notice how many of the children are barefoot, their soles dirty, as they, caught up in the excitement, slide and scamper around the polished airport floor.

A man with a board is waiting for him at the exit. He is holding a large white card, MR ALAN MANSANI. Alan will steer his trolley towards that man who, seeing Alan, will approach, nodding. 'Mr Alan Mansani? I am Joseph Mensa. I am a great admirer of your father's work. Welcome home.'

A Sea Point widower speaks

The lift doors open but Reuben Solomon stands outside, for the moment suddenly, though not unexpectedly, paralysed by fear. He had already made up his mind, decided, that he would get in, only now he is not so sure. What if the lift *does* stall with him still inside, hanging in thin air in this metal coffin between the tenth and basement floors? It is possible. It happened just recently to a maid working for one of the families in the block, she was trapped for five hours in the pitch dark. Eskom power cuts. Now they say they will give prior warning, but how do you know that they mean what they say? Trust, that is not a word these people understand. Organisation. They couldn't organise a picnic.

No no no. Not to live like this, always fearful, a hardening fossil, old age turning your life to stone. He steps in, presses the ground floor button, watches the doors close. Prison.

4. They must do *something* about the state of this lift, he thinks. An upgrade. *3.* Refurbishment, back-up power, something, something in case of – *2.* – another sudden power failure. The technology must exist nowadays. If not, it should. He will talk to Cyril, someone on the management board. *1.* Agh, what will they do about it? Probably nothing. How long have the letters CA been missing from the sign outside? Ca/margue. Morgue. He must speak to someone in the committee. He still pays his property rates and building levies. Can't just be allowed to get away blue murder, incompetence. Aged lungs and hearts wouldn't last fifteen minutes in this pilchard tin if it ever juddered to a halt.

The doors ping open. Reuben steps outside. Relief. Disaster avoided, for the moment. So maybe it will all be all right. Maybe all the worry is only in his mind, he thinks, as he soft-shoes up the ramp and through the automatic glass doors, gestures acknowledgement to Niels on security, outside into the spring sunshine and salty, bracing sea air. But he must try to at least *talk* to Cyril about doing something. She would have; would have made them make provision for the power cuts.

Of course when they bought this flat and first moved in here, into the Camargue building on Beach Road, Sea Point in 1971, it was considered solid gold bricks-and-mortar real estate. Very exclusive with its uninterrupted ocean views, a beautiful vista, First World, top notch. I can see the sea, see the sea, see the sea – the song that later their grandchildren visiting from rainy London, England sang as they examined their grandmother's collection of quartz and other semiprecious stones on the glass coffee table. And she, she loved this view, always. Every day different, the blue crests and little white frothy folds. And the sunsets – exotic colours like the feathers of tropical birds. All sorts of things she noticed, all those little details for her paintings. She in front of the window in the breakfast nook, in front of the window, standing behind her easel with her apron over her house clothes. Wooden palette in one hand, smeared with paint. Struggling between Carmelite Red, Orchard

Orange, Silver Grey, wanting to get it just right. 'Because it's something oh so lovely, isn't it, Reuben.'

Eventually she gave up. Paint brushes left to dry out and go brittle. Pastels too, and the oils. Just too perfect and lovely for her clumsy, talentless hands to capture, she said, hard on herself always. But generous with others.

They should be here any moment, his two daughters Sharon and Valerie, hooting for him. That's why it is better to be a few minutes early, he feels and always tells himself, to save on hype and stress levels later. Valerie, she is the worst the worst the worst. Running around the place, shooting here shooting there, a regular ping-pong ball of frenzied activity that can't stay still for more than ten minutes, it seems, as if it's *her* clock that is winding down. As if *she* is the one that has maybe only six (ten, tops) Septembers left.

Here come the Feinsteins. 'Yes, fine, thank you. Waiting for my daughters. The hip, Ruth? Okay? And the diabetes, Joseph? That's right. That's what my doctor keeps on telling me. Exercise, exercise. Well, bye bye.'

It is not easy being a widower amongst all of this, Reuben thinks mournfully as he watches the Feinsteins, arm hooked through liver-spotted arm, each one buoying the other like two cripples as they cross the road for their early morning hobble, breathing their way along the seafront. She'd died at the end of the old time in South Africa, before the new had really begun, and left him to deal with all of this kak alone. Why don't you get a dog, Pa? Lionel's words from his busy actuary office in London. A dog? Do you think that will take care of it?, Reuben thought to himself scornfully when Lionel suggested it. My son says I should get a dog. He wanted things to stay as they were, as they had been before, couldn't Lionel understand? Why don't you take

73

the stickers off the cupboards and drawers, Pa? It's been ten years, you know where everything is now, what you want to keep them for? Because she put them there, that's why. She had worried he would have trouble. She tried to take care of everything as she had always done. But if she could see it now, if she could only see it. Claremont Kosher is still there. Simon's was long closed. Lily's. Ellerslie is now a school for, he doesn't know, mentally retarded black children, that's how they look to him when he passes them all gathered outside on his way to the post office at the Adelphi Centre. Not enough teenage Jewish girls left, maybe with all the young families emigrating, to keep two Jewish high schools in the city going. Once there were three, four.

There was no denying it, from top hat to shabby heel, the standards in the city and across the entire country were in free fall. And those things that weren't toppling, well, they were no longer affordable. How the poor are managing, he doesn't know. Schwartzers screwing their own. That's how it always goes in Africa – Zimbabwe, Nigeria, greed, corruption, greed. To watch SABC3 news, to read the papers, he almost can't bear to do it. He buys the *Cape Times* for the crossword, but then his eyes wander and before you know it, a quagmire of doom doom. Death, a ticking time bomb of bad news. And now a turtle-faced dancing schmuck steering the ship. Good thing she is not alive to see it, she would have taken it to heart. All those years of handing out pamphlets for Helen Suzman and the Progressive Party, he remembers it well. She ignored all his warnings, all of them. For *goodness* sake, Esti, at least put the flyers in your purse until you make your drops, even a blind Nat could see what you're carrying: South Africa Needs Change and Now. Think, Esti, think! Arrest, detention, torture, solitary confinement. Look what happened to Ruth First! Think! But she never worried. Always the optimist, seeing only the good in people, seeing the hope.

Agh, what for? Only to carry the burden of disappointments later? If she could see what they have done to this very beachfront promenade. As nice, once, he has heard, as Buenos Aires when it was still the classy apple of South America's jet-set eye. As nice as something similar in the South of France, in Nice. As nice as Nice and the Promenade Anglaise, his own children sent him a picture once, maybe better in its heyday. And now? If he cocks his head and takes a glance in the direction of the creeping Feinsteins, enough to raise a person's blood pressure to Cooked. Over there beside the jungle gym and swings, them, lying on the grass. Canoodling couples, tramps. That big black lady with the shopping trolley and plastic bags, he went to go talk to her once. Took her some food, as he thought she would have done for him. The schwartzer snatched it from his trembling hands, not even a thank you, not even an acknowledgement. They think every little thing just comes, that the white has *got* to give it to them. Though she would say, Oh Reuben, maybe it's not her fault, maybe she was embarrassed or afraid. And she has definitely had a hard life. Why would a woman want to live like that? Must be dangerous for her, all alone on this promenade at night. And cold. Something must have happened to her to make her like that. Like she said when he caught that employee, that coloured chappie Richards, with his hand in the till at the shop. Oh Reuben, think of his wife, his children, something must be going on at home, he must have needed the extra money. Maybe one of the children is sick. No, Esti, a thief is a thief, a bad egg is a bad egg. For some people, it's in their blood, that's what you've got to understand. Not everybody is as good as you, you must accept it.

When he sees her today, he won't tell her any of this. He has a rule for the graveside: no politics. He will keep it personal, as he always does. When the girls go to find the tombstone of their grandmother, her mother, they have a little chat, talk about this and about that, how the girls are really getting on, family worries and intimacies that married couples share. Not too many worries though. So many personal things that he really wants to say, of course, he won't. Like, how come you left me like this, Esti? Why couldn't you wait a little longer until my engine was running down too? You took too good care of me, that's the problem. Always feeding me well, all that emphasis on green vegetables, carbohydrates, lean cuts of meat – every meal divided into five. Everything picked up in books – the Good Food Diet for Your Family.

And exercise. How she loved to walk, along this very beachfront, thinks Reuben, all the way to Camps Bay and back. To dance, going dancing every Saturday night with their friends, ballroom, dressed up to the nines. People then still knew something about how to conduct themselves. No jeans. Hats and gloves. Sundays a drive in the car with the children to get clean air into their lungs. Not just along the coast – Hermanus, into the mountains, Tokai Forest, that they should know the smell of pine, the sight of a real growing mushroom, the names of some wild flowers. That they should be more rounded individuals.

Now, of course, there is no time for that. Lionel shifting shares and juggling figures in London, divorced at fifty-seven, again the man about town. Both girls busy with trying to build relationships with their children and grandchildren thousands of miles away, Skyping them; it's like the telephone, Pa, only cheaper and you use the internet, and we can see their faces too, through a little camera. *What*? Oh all right, as long as it works. When they come here for holidays once every two, three years, they don't take them to the forest. Too dangerous, they say. Or to the beaches. Filthy, crawling with blacks or worse, tourists. Muizenberg? Pah! The worst. The very very worst. Syringes in the sand, druggie immigrants, sharks hungry for human flesh.

They do have a point, Reuben thinks to himself. You can see the problem, if you stand here, close to the curb. Sure, there are lots of normal people around, ordinary people, young people, housewives jogging or walking their dogs up and down, to and from Mouille Point Lighthouse. But you can't deny it, can't ignore it. Over there, the grizzled yellow grass. Yellow from what? Drought, sure, but also urine. Urine, human excrement. These people, these blacks, lying around in the sun, even though it is ten in the morning and they should be at least looking for gainful employment, they urinate on it. Squat and do number twos. He has seen it with his own eyes, and as Cyril said last week at bridge, 'Who knows how things will go when Mandela finally dies. Did you see him on television last night? He looks old. *Old*. If he has four more years left, he'd be lucky. We'd all be lucky. What then? Two spades. Then will come, my friend, the great bloody revolution.'

God, Esti, all your hard work for this, Reuben says out loud, squinting into the sun towards heaven. What she did not do, the meetings she did not attend, the liberals she did not befriend. That moffie and his boyfriend – the artist with his crazy paintings about District Six and one man, one vote. Even now she would do something about the lift, wouldn't just take it lying down, Reuben thinks, as he watches Mrs Meyer with her coloured carer entering the lift, potential victims in a Venus flytrap of crushing metal and claustrophobic darkness.

And the cemetery in Pinelands, what about that? He does not like what they have done to Pinelands. It was never a beautiful place, granted, but there was grass and some shrubs around the graves. That is why she chose it, that and because both her parents are buried there, may they rest in peace. Yes, there were flowers, though it is not the Jewish way, not like the Christians to lavish a grave as though it were a wedding or a Sandton dinner party supper table. Stone. That is what you get. Stone and stone and now concrete to keep out, they say, the grave robbers after the coffin wood.

Should drive himself, Reuben thinks. To not be a burden on the children, to keep some independence, the brain's juices gurgling. But now a man who once in his youth and with his wife's encouragement swam, danced, played golf, fished, and de-scaled and gutted those fish himself, those that she didn't make him throw back into the water – that such a man should end up a number on the school run, chaperoned everywhere. Taken to the Pick 'n Pay supermarket at the Waterfront mall once a week on his one daughter's insistence to choose groceries, shaving cream, soap and polish for the maid. And by the other to doctors, dentists, bridge on a Wednesday night. 'That's how bones start to rattle, Reuben. That's how we turn to dust.' What next? Soiled nappies like Jeremy Bloom. Agh, it could make you hate yourself and your ageing body, its great conspiracy against you. Better to go quickly, from disease, like she did. A bit younger, all your faculties together, in one lucid piece.

But it isn't only his daughters. He knows, he knows, though he doesn't like to admit it: Fear. The same fear as kept him lingering a few moments ago outside the open lift door like a dithering geriatric. He doesn't *like* going out on his own any more. Anything might happen. And as for driving, he is intimidated by the traffic on the roads these days. Driving around Cape Town – why not driving in a grand prix? Through a zoo? Cameroon? The black minibus taxi drivers, lethal weapons – each one bought his licence over a table in a shebeen, never sat a test. Yes, for sure.

Truth is, he isn't ready to die, not yet. He is afraid of it, a little afraid, still. 'I didn't lead such a righteous life as you, my dear Esti. There, I said it. And is it possible while you went straight up I maybe taking the lift to someplace else? You never know, it is possible. Is ours not after all a vengeful God? Isn't that what the Great Scroll says?'

There – the car. They are here.

Sharon smiling opens the backseat door for him. How are you? Everything okay, Pa? He should reply as usual. All the mendacity of polite trivial conversation, like talking to the Feinsteins: Fine, Good, Never better. But no, instead when he gets in the car and his daughters ask him *'Are you okay, Pa?'* it might just come out naked, come out raw – the truth. All the weary bitterness and loneliness of this life, finally exposed by his words and his tone for them to see, acknowledge and digest.

THE RED EARTH

*D*o you know about TB, Mrs Sithole? Okay, you know about it. Well, because of her Aids, your daughter now has a serious TB infection. And because she has Aids, her body isn't fighting this TB infection the way we'd want it to. According to our tests, yes, it's unfortunately not yet responded to our course of treatment. That's why your daughter's still so sick, so weak. She needs more, another few months of different treatments. We cannot be certain…

I look into the face of this young doctor. I envy it, fat and healthy like it is. Her hand holding the wooden clipboard with the sheets of paper on it, it is plump and strong. It could do anything that she asked of it. She is not looking at me as she speaks about me. She is only looking down at her pieces of paper, looking at one, then another, then the one on top, her mouth and nose covered with one of their cloth masks. I do not want to listen any more. I turn to look at my mother, who is standing next to my bed. She is wearing a mask too, but in her bright colours, yellow and green, she is like a piece of our home village, a single shoot of bright summer mealies amongst all these cold iron hospital beds and cement walls. Mama, I want to whisper, Mama, I want to go home.

Behind her mask this doctor's mouth is still moving. It moves it moves. I imagine plump, soft lips – I too used to have such lips, white strong teeth that can chew meat, tongue without any sores, body clean of disease. I look again at the old woman, my mother, who has travelled so far to come and visit me in this place today. I want to go home, Mama, that is what I want.

But I cannot go home. I know I am not allowed. The breath of those like me is, according to this doctor and the nurses of this hospital, a kind of poison and it can spread through the air without even being seen. Anyway, I am too weak to walk. These useless legs of mine are carrying me nowhere for the moment. So tired. And when I breathe... *yo*. Constant fire, bubbling cooking oil in my chest. Cough too. Yes, sure sure, but also the stomach sickness, diarrhoea and swelling caused by so many months of painful injections, and in the end, as this doctor has just admitted to my Mama, they are still useless. Mama, how long? How long have I already lain here like so, a lame dog? Five months, four, or is it already six? I do not know. Every day is just the same for us who live here. After treatment we feel so bad that we forget whether it is day or night or week or weekend. We forget that life used to go forward, that once we did feel strong. What we need is a big clock, high on the wall, just to *know* for certain that time is passing, understand? Just to *know*. Look, she cannot hear me, my Mama. She is listening, listening to what this doctor is telling her. That is right, Mama. Your daughter, she is not going home. She is not.

A nurse is approaching. She always moves so slowly, this one, when the doctors call. It is like watching a lazy storm cloud move across the winter sky. I have watched and heard her, heard her speaking loudly, complaining to the other one, the small one with the large backside. *Yo!* She says, these patients are too demanding, these doctors arrogant with all their orders for us. We are only two, two to serve twenty helpless patients, real grown babies. Yo yo! Two pairs of hands. If they want more from us, they must operate, cut us in half! This nurse, she is gliding closer now. She has brought her trolley with her to take my temperature. Her anger, it is like a porcupine's sharp coat of thorns, it is a thorn under my skin. Why should I look at her? I ask myself. I still have my pride. This great baboon is no friend of mine. Instead I close my eyes, swallow. Pain, fire, raging all over my body. Especially here, where I breathe and when I breathe. And the doctor? Still talking. Words, so many words, talk and talk, talk. Exhausts me. Her bad news, it exhausts me. If only to die in peace, I think. But no, that is not how it is going to be.

'Open your mouth, Bongumusa, open.' It is the angry nurse. Obediently, but with a great effort, I must open for her. 'Wider, wider.' To make room for the long glass thermometer that in my mind is worse than a sangoma's spear being thrust into a helpless ox. Everything hurts, understand. My tongue. To be touched, even to be held with the greatest tenderness. This morning when my mother washed me with the basin of warm water I thought I would cry each time the sponge brushed my skin. For a moment now, my tongue will throb like it has been struck hard, stabbed deep. But I will not show my mother how much her only daughter suffers. She looks, smiles, thinks such things can make me feel better.

I close my eyes. I taste the spear's hot metal. 'Closed, keep it closed. Now open.' I must open it again. This nurse stands. See how bored she looks, bored for all to see. My Mama cannot look at her. See how one fat arm is folded across her large chest and with the other hand she is holding the thermometer with my temperature on it, holding it out to this doctor as though it alone could kill. The doctor looks at it, nods, scribbles something down on her pad. That is right, yes, I know all of their actions already, know them by heart. Now the nurse must wipe it clean. Ha! Clean from me as though these are the old days and I have just given birth and so everything that I touch is now considered dirty. She does this with a tissue. Watch: the tissue and thermometer she will drop into her bucket of disinfectant on her trolley. She will peel off her plastic gloves and drop them in the bucket too. See, she does it just like I say, and takes her trolley and without another word pushes it away and is gone.

Mama, what are you thinking? I can see that you are frowning. You look confused, what are you thinking Mama? I am not the first one that you have watched, not so? How many now? Four. Before me your son-in-law and two older sons. First Fula, soon after Buyisana, then my Sipho. Each one the same story, was it not so, Mama? As ugly as I have become, this body of mine down to its loose skin and its sharp bones.

I know, Mama, I helped to care for them too, remember? And watched them as you now watch me, life slipping through like delicate sand blown away more and more each day until nothing is left. We could do nothing for them, hey Mama. Not even expensive goat's blood medicines. It is true. They are buried now, I can still see the place very clearly. I visit it often in my mind. I leave this useless body of mine and fly down the steep south-facing hill at the back of the house where their graves are marked by small wooden crosses in the red earth.

When the wind comes up from the valley through the village, does it still blows the crosses down, Mama, and do you still send Nomusa to replace them? You should not, she does not like it. She is superstitious, the other children have said things to her in school. You should send Mbimbi.

I have never told you, Mama, but when the fever has been very bad in this place I have had some messages from my brothers and from my husband. They have visited me three times already in my dreams. They have told me: our mighty ancestor's blood that was spilt, the earth drank it, that is why the soil is red. That red earth now also becomes our graves. Soon the earth will grow redder and redder with all the bodies that are being put into it and soon everyone will be able to smell the blood, like wet metal, like rust, like you can smell it when you have slaughtered a goat or an ox. See that one lying next door? That young woman very sick in that bed with her family all around, mother, aunties, sisters? She is dying, I mean she is almost dead. They rest hands on the lumps on the blankets that used to mean her hand, leg, foot. They do not know, but she knows. You know my sissy, hey, I know you do. Know about the blood in the earth. Know what I am talking about? Yes?

One year ago, since ARVs, before this TB, my own death and my grave felt very far away. A year ago what could I still do? Though still I had the Aids, since the tablets, I believed I could conquer it myself and I would conquer it, not only in my own body, understand, but also in all the places of my village and in the surrounding towns too. I wore a t-shirt given to me to wear by one of the charities that came to speak with patients like myself one day at the Aids clinic: HIV-positive. They convinced me to participate in one of their awareness parades and I did it. I could dance, could clap, could stamp my feet and stir the dust. I could sing, could throw my voice towards the sky and watch it roll from hill to hill like thunder and then fall, entering the ears of anyone willing to listen. I had a good singing voice, you know. At one such event one year ago, I remember, I led the singing group. And always in church, I sang at the end and start of the services. The minister would say, 'Sing, Sissy! Sing! Stand up and let the angels celebrate! For Jesus is coming!' My fine singing is gone now, coughed and vomited out.

Before, in the beginning, before the charity with the singing and the songs, I fought back at the people in my village who called women like myself names because they had heard the disease, the Aids, came from having sex with many men while our husbands were away working in the cities. Some women, the people even attacked them with machetes. To see what they did to them, how they hurt them! Because they wanted them driven from their villages, from their towns. Driven out. They thought that they were cursed because that is what some sangomas had said.

But I was courageous, I am telling you now. I had already buried my brothers and my husband. Do not just sit down quietly to die and do nothing, that is what I told myself. Remember Queen Nandi, warrior mother of the great King Shaka. No one would speak of it, but I spoke of it. No one would come near me, to my house, or let me close, but I went to them. Now, more and more often, I have heard from Mama, through the streets of the big towns we know there are awareness parades like I used to sing in before, and in squares, in community youth centres bare as bread, community HIV/Aids drama. So some things are getting better? Yes? I tell myself Yes even though in my heart I am not so sure. Last spring my own children participated in one such spectacle for those with parents and family sick and dying from HIV/Aids. The government posters in the schools and along the tarred roads, they say education can save my children. Save them from death because of the virus. But what can save them from this? And who can save them? A life without mother or father?

These doctors and nurses, they do not really know what to do with us, I know this. They lock us in here like animals, put on their masks and tell us, 'Here, take, take these medicines, take.' So many. But I am not feeling better. 'You will.' Sicker than before. 'Trust, it will come. Now come, we are not giving you these for our own good, hey? Yo! Very expensive, understand? Now come come come, swallow. Give me your arm your leg so I can put this needle into you.' And the ARVs. No good for the TB, so they are no good but still I take, two times every day. 'Take them too. Come come come. Do not take so long. Swallow, swallow.'

Since the TB has come, there is only that. It has brought with it new things I know. The ARVs, they had made things once again possible for me for eleven months, but now it is again completely impossible. Just to walk by myself, anywhere. Using the toilet without help. And sitting up. Eating solid foods, bread, meat, all that I enjoyed before. I can no longer take milk, chew, sing, talk. Words. Finding the words to talk about things, and even those things seem to be slipping further and further away from me every morning, my real life growing as thin as my body.

I do not know. Do not ask me any more about hope or no hope, I do not know. Yes, it is true, I do still believe in miracles. My name, does it not mean 'She who can put her trust in God'? She who can trust the ancestors, Jesus

Christ? They saved me once, from the Aids, made me feel strong again. I could look after my children, could work for them and hold them, could work for the charity. Still now, still now, so close to the end, so sick, I do pray. First to Jesus Christ, then to the mighty ancestors, finally to my own body. But do they have the power to save me again?

I will tell you a secret, the secret of what I pray to my body each morning. 'Listen, body, I pray, listen to me well. I will look after you if you will look after me. I will be good to you if you are good to me too, if you give me power and help me to fight and kill this new disease as our ancestors once slaughtered their enemies. Please, give me the strength to do it. If you keep me strong and healthy so that I can care for my children and protect them, then I will look after you and care for you and never spoil you.' But I do not know if my body can even hear me any more, that is the truth. All I now know is this pain, this fire inside that cannot be put out, and the feeling that I am only just managing to hang on, too scared for the moment to let go. Not for myself, understand. No, for my three children, that is why I fight, that is why I stay here and hope and try. I need to think of my children, understand. To know that first they will be all right. The girls? I hope and pray that they will they be safe. I know they are sensible. They listen to their grandmother, they go to church, they take care with their school studies. But the boy... only four, too young. The difficult question is, have I put enough into them, into my two girls, taught them enough over these thirteen years, to help them with their younger brother when I am no longer here?

I do not have the strength at the moment to offer my daughters and my son any more lessons. Only to lie here and to breathe and to breathe and to breathe. Each shallow burning breath is a decision to not give up yet. So I hang on for them, to them, my three children. I'm a day trapped, caught, waiting for the sun to set finally or to rise again. Doctor, hey? What do you say? Which will it be?

And you, Mama? I look at you again and again, Mama. You too will not live forever. This morning when you arrived I saw how you have grown very old and tired with all your grief these past years. A woman your age should have many children to take care of her, but instead you are forced to take care of them, your grandchildren too. And the journey? That journey where you carried me here, your grown daughter, to this town's clinic on your back like a baby, was very hard for you. You had to stop many times. If the bakkie had not come along offering us a lift, I am not sure either of us would have made it. I miss my home, Mama. I miss seeing people's whole faces without masks, the faces of those that I love.

But I am not dead, not dead quite yet. Better, stronger still than the dying girl next door. Uncle's buffalo thorn waits. It waits to call my soul back to our homestead. So there are still some things I can do, not so? I still have some choices left. For example, I can choose to lie here quietly, shivering in my body, and decide whether or not I will love it or I will hate it. Sometimes I cannot help it, you know, I love it still, in spite of everything, in spite of how useless it has become, when I remember what my body could do before, how it once was. This morning when I caught sight of my right hand as my mother was washing my fingers gently with the sponge, like clay pottery that might break, I remembered my old self. These hands, that today I can hardly move beneath the sheet, that sometimes will not even hold a cup, they were once beautiful hands, hands with a mind, always busy cooking, carrying, clapping, caressing, sweeping, sewing. These feet walked, stomped, danced. I cannot move my toes, I cannot. But sometimes in my mind I am still performing all those actions that my body now refuses to do and at such times I also wonder if we need bodies at all. No body and you are like the wind – everywhere, free. Only, the wind is lonely too. That is why sometimes it cannot help itself but it must howl. Not last night or today, all is quiet. But sometimes it howls so loudly outside this hospital, I tell you, or tears at people's houses in my village, ripping at our roofs, shaking the hinges of doors and windows, trying to force its way in through the mud, the brick, the grooves, so that it can be with us, touch us, if only for a short while; so no one can deny how lonely the wind really is.

Death, it is lonely, yes. This hospital, a lonely lonely place even with so many other sick people around, shivering and moaning, stinking of our own sweat mixed with the hospital disinfectant. The plump, healthy white and brown faces of the doctors and nurses seem to be in the wrong place. They are the strangers here, the living amongst us pale sweating ghosts. I and the others male and female, young and old, brothers and sisters, of a single, outcast tribe yet each alone, apart. Each alone and apart in his own suffering, understand. I tell you something more, when we catch another's eye, my fellow patients and I, we look without interest. Why be interested? We know that face, know it too well, it is our own.

Everything dies. That is what you learn if you lie in bed all day with nothing to do but look out through the locked window or watch the sick growing only sicker with each new full moon. Everything comes to its end – daylight, sun, night, rain. The plants grow then wither, the food is cooked then eaten, words are spoken then disappear into memory and are eventually forgotten, you are given hope – you will get better, you will be healed – and then it is taken. And my children? What will become of them? Of their lives? I know that once I am gone there will be arguments about my children. Mama tells me the fighting has already started with my brother's wife. I want my mother to keep them but who will listen once I am no longer alive? Not for love, understand. They do not want them because of love but because of the government money grants for orphans. If I think about this too long, if I let myself think on it, God, I am suddenly so very, very angry, so it gives me a spasm, a pain deep deep inside my chest. The fire roars. I taste blood. Then I want to hit, to strike, to bite, to scream and throw myself from this damn bed and run, fall out of this hospital, die on the road back to my village if I have to, because a child, it needs its mother.

I must push myself up. I cannot just be lying here, silent as a lump of stone, a lame dog, any longer while you speak, doctor, I am going home, I am going. To hell with you, doctor. I try to get up, to push myself up but I can only bare my teeth, moan. Yo. She is looking at me now, oooh, yo, she looks very worried, her eyes. No, don't touch me! Don't! Her mouth, what is it saying behind her mask? Now they are coming, taking their time, moving slowly from the other end of the room beside the door. They are shouting something at Mama. Go to school! Don't go to school! Take your schoolbooks, throw them into the stove! Get out! They are shouting at my children back home in my village, Go!

Yes, that is it, that is right! I am upset. But I do not need to rest. No! The doctor is taking Mama, but where? From this room. I watch her, my mother, an old woman swept away with her bag of beans picked for me from the red soil of my people, soil full of blood from bodies and birth-cords and the birth-cords of my own children and all we have already buried, my children too. I watch them all go and see them all, Mama and my children, my husband and my brothers swallowed by a black hole. Soon soon, a country of orphans, soon soon. The nurses are coming, the cloud who passes without knowing what a heavy shadow she casts, the other little one too. Faces like angry farm dogs, both. Their strong hands will push me down and back into this pillow. Their masked mouths will issue me with stern warnings about my health and the health of these other patients. And I am so ungrateful, they cannot believe it. Oh go to hell, man, don't you know we are dying? What have we to be grateful for? I must tell them, I must let these nurses know.

I feel like an orphan myself, understand. Completely alone, that is how I feel. My own children no longer belong to me. My own mother no longer belongs to me. My own body no longer belongs to me. I am an orphan, understand? Apart from everything, everyone.

THE DICTIONARY

Imagine if you can, my friend. You are a man on your back in thick blackness. It is midnight – or rather, you *think* it is midnight. Many years ago they confiscated your wrist watch along with all other personal possessions and tender tokens and so you have no way of knowing for certain whether it is really midnight or not. You take matters into your own hands. You decide, it *is* midnight. You are awake. You have been trying to fall asleep for what seems like hours and know that now, in all probability, you will not sleep. In such circumstances you know too that you will be unable to run from the memories of your past for long.

For men like myself in Pretoria Central the past is very painful, who can deny that? So forgive me if perhaps I try to delay its presence for another few moments. A trick I have taught myself – focus the mind on simple, present realities.

So, tonight. What can I tell you only of tonight, 12 January 1988? A night like every other in this place and yet like no other. Haai, too many reasons. You yourself awake, the rest asleep. For example, Xela, your Xhosa neighbour on your right, as soon as his head touches his jacket, he is off. And David, your Venda comrade on your left side, snoring in your ear as loud as an ox. Every night he roars like this. What else? Come come. This oppressive darkness, you alone in it – that is your feeling – not one of many, in spite of all these bodies crushed together around you like so many bony Transkei cattle – but an island. And? This familiar uncontrollable desire, no, *need*, real grave need, to talk.

What else? Tonight Zola does not grind his teeth in his sleep in the bed opposite. Tonight the water pipes in this place do not rattle with rust and old age. Tonight I can hear nothing in the passage. No sound of warders' squeaking leather boots pacing and then stopping, listening at our door. Not a bored sjambok being dragged absent-mindedly along the wall. Tonight this large chamber is very cool. For sure tonight there is a new brutal coolness in the air, so I ask myself, has autumn come to umhlaba ngaphandle – the world outside? This morning as I lined up with the other men along the passage, waiting for permission like little children to go to the toilet block, we felt sure that it was creeping towards us along the concrete floor, making our skin underneath our cotton clothes go goosefleshed so that we had no choice but to huddle together as close as possible.

But of course I have no way of knowing for certain whether autumn has really come or not. And this is how they want it, right? To try to keep us blind and completely ignorant. No books, no newspapers, mo magazines, no television, no radio, no trips outside. I have been here long enough to know the rules. Rules say, thirty minutes once a day, forty men at one time, take exercise in the recreation yard. But in reality, and this is no joke man, we have not been allowed out of this block once these past fifteen months. It is because of the *threat* of violence, they tell us. There were some squabbles, some gangster got stabbed in another block two years ago. You are prisoners, they say, we will decide what is good for you. Ha ha. I laugh and they now look very serious. Their smiles slide off like melted butter, their voices are dangerous like electricity, their sjamboks ready to sail through the air and strike. 'You are not here to laugh and makes jokes, kaffir.'

That has always been my trouble. I do not know how to keep quiet, I admit it, that is what brought me to this prison in the first place – words, language, a book. Ha! If I told you how, you would not believe me.

So my story. Whether I am ready for it, or you are ready for it, it doesn't matter. It is coming now whether we want it to or not. So so so. Go back fourteen years. I too was the white man's monkey. Each day, five thirty, I jump out of bed to collect and boil some water on the stove and wash with a face cloth in the tin basin in the middle of my room on newspaper so as not to wet the floor in front of my wardrobe. Hurry hurry. Then I pull on my underwear, my shirt, my socks, my jacket with black buttons, my pair of gray pants, my polished black shoes, my cap. Then I run to catch two buses to Webber Steel Company – a two-hour journey from the place where I live. It's a building in the very heart of Johannesburg city, very grand and tall, a glass tower stretching up and up like an elegant transparent neck into the pale blue sky.

I was watchman. *Deurmens.* I sat at a small desk in the entrance so that no one could pass by without first passing me. At that desk I watched through the glass as the whole world of downtown Jo'burg hurried about, performing its very urgent business. It was my job to open the door for the white people and to accept packages, also to run errands. And if someone came wanting to shoot or rob them, it was my place to die first. I was good at my job, a very good watchman. Only you see, my friend, there was a problem. Every morning for five years, I let the employees in. Very educated-looking people, in sharp suits with ties and carrying briefcases, bundles of important papers and documents.

'Boy!' I was nearly twenty-five when I started my employment with them, a man, circumcised with a wife and four children back home. 'Come!'

'Yes, Baas Sir?'

'Can't you see I'm struggling here?'

'Yes, sorry, Sir.'

'Carry these upstairs.'

How many stairs? Two hundred stairs, seventh floor. 'Certainly, Sir.' Off I went whilst Baas took the lift. Then back downstairs fast, sweat pouring, mopping it with a handkerchief, to open the door for the next.

'Boy!'

'Ja, Baas Sir?'

'I need something from the car. Here are my keys.'

'Yes, Baas. No problem, Sir.'

Those serious faces very proud. The women too, the secretaries, with their red lipstick and swinging handbags. I ran for them, but not once in five years did those same white people greet me or even thank me for all my sweat.

Really I knew why not. I know the truth, that the black man in the city is no different from the black man in the provinces, the white man thinks of us only as a pair of hands and strong, fast legs, tools. If he needs something carried or cleaned, that is for us. And we let him. I mean *I* let him. I played my part perfectly for the first thirty years of my life and for my first five years at Webber Steel Company.

But then one day, I do not know, I thought to myself, sekwanele manje, enough is enough, something must change. Me, perhaps I could learn to stomach it. In five years I had not so far managed to, but maybe in ten or twelve years, twenty more years, who knows? But what about my children? End of each month, on the 29th, I sent my wages home. And a letter: 'Give the kids their father's love, Gabisile. Make sure they keep going to school.' It was my plan that my four daughters would one day have a very different life from me. Because of this dream I already made many sacrifices. I lived in just one room. I allowed myself very few luxuries – some cigarettes, on Friday nights a few beers at the shebeen with my friends, and once a month a ticket to the bioscope to watch those American gangster films. Seventy percent of my salary each month I sent home to my wife with her parents in kwaDuakuza so that the children and she could be well fed, have decent clothes and proper shoes, and my kids, they could go to school. But what good is an education if you know that in the end they will not be permitted to use it?

Okay, I need a short break. It is not, you see, my friend, an enviable task, to choose between the unbearable realities of the present or the unbearable losses and memories of the past.

Let me leave the past, just for a moment. I will tell you another story, another story about here and now. Some of the prisoners want to compose a letter. Give us schooling, we are not animals. Teach us trades, skills. Instead, what? Instead they give us this – blackness. To match our black skins, a perfect recipe for misery and for invisibility. Where is the hope, the compassion? No one wants to know what really brought us here. Locked away in this place we are forgotten by those on the outside who want to see us buried in this prison, alive but dead. Understand?

What was I saying? Ngikhliwe ukuthi dengicadangani. That's right, I didn't know what I would do. All I knew was that after five years but really thirty years, and who am I bluffing, three hundred and fifty years before that, ever since the white man first set foot on this land, I was fed up and somehow I knew I had to teach these whites a lesson. I waited, as they say, for a revelation about what I could do.

One day, when I was waiting for the second bus to transport me home, I saw it sitting in the window of a shop that sold knick-knacks and second-hand odds and ends. There in the window it was – dark blue Concise Oxford Dictionary. I do not know why – because I am a practical man, you see, and knew in my life there was very little use for books – but I wanted this book with great yearning. I went inside and convinced the Indian who owned the shop to let me have it for six rand, paid off fifty cents a month for six months, and I left my wristwatch with him as a guarantee – the same one that they took from me when they brought me here.

The day I took it home was a very proud day. I sat on my bed and opened it and suddenly my very small room seemed very large and for the first time, looking out the window, I did not see miles of shit, places like mine and no further possibilities. I saw a future. You see, I knew what

I would do to change this country. I would educate the white man in his own language about his own language. For us Africans, you know, words are not just words, they really mean something. If you say 'brother' you mean it. 'Love', 'hate', 'forgiveness', these are not empty shadows, they speak for us. I had decided the whites were not bad at heart, they were just never very good at languages. isiZulu, isiXhosa, siSwati, forget it! Even his own language – he had forgotten half the words that existed in his own language – or forgotten their meanings, words such as 'compassion', 'feeling', 'charity', 'generosity', 'equality'. I knew with the help of the dictionary I would discover many more. I felt it my duty, not just for myself but for my children, to try and remind him.

I began with a word most white people seem to have forgotten, especially when it comes to dealing with a black man, 'manners'. The next morning after taking the dictionary home, I arrived for work, seven o'clock as usual. When the first white swept past me without so much as a 'Good morning' I began, with a flourish. Not with 'Good morning, Mr Baas' or 'Good day, Mr Baas Brown' or 'Goeie môre, Mev Madam Kimton.' I made a point of showing them what their own language could do. Vigorously that morning and all the mornings that followed, I made the first gracious move: 'Salutations! May today be a day of richness for you and your fair family.' They looked at me strangely – it is true – with confused looks on their proud faces. Here was some kaffir man using such big words, who does the monkey think he is? But my plan was not a failure. I had got their attention and I learnt that given time and with some patience they were not such poor students. They began to greet me as they hurried past clutching briefcases or bundles of documents, though still did not look at me or address me as Mr Ndlela.

So? I am a patient man. Several more days passed. I made a policy, to memorise fifteen new important English words each day. This was not too difficult. Sometimes many hours would go past without the single appearance of a potential client for Webber Steel Company. I started with the Letter A. It was Tuesday. By the following Tuesday, I was on the letter C.

I had not expected to discover so many words the whites had seemingly forgotten. In Cs alone, I found: Compassion, Consideration, Communication, Connection, Conspecific, Console, Christian, Congenial, Comfort, Concourse, Conciliate, Concatenate, Conceited, Compromise, Compunction, Comrade, Contumelious, Contumely, Convention, Converge, Conversation, Converse, Cooperate, Cordial. One day it was very quiet in the glass skyscraper and I was reading the dictionary. I found a word that I liked very much. It was certainly important. That day I found as many opportunities to use it as was possible. So when the messenger came – a man who was always very rude, treating me with great disrespect, even contempt – with a parcel for the Big Baas, I said, 'That red of your bag, in some cultures I have heard it said it is the colour of contrition.'

Ha ha, that rude messenger did not know how to respond to such truth telling as that, it was better than if I had punched him in the stomach. His check puffed out like a plastic bag full of wind and his face went red as a tomato. He flung the parcel across the desk and left. Outside, his motorbike blew up the street with a belch. And when he came two days later, he was reasonable, saying, even, 'Thank you.'

Time passed, perhaps a month. Things were now no longer going according to my plans, I began to notice. The more I read the dictionary – the more words from English I found it pertinent to remind my white employers of – the more angry the whites around me grew. They were regressing, that is for sure.

I was taken aback. I knew I had to correct this unimpressive attitude of animosity and amnesia as quickly as possible. I made a dramatic gesture. One day, when the Big Baas man, Mr Peters, swung past me without so much as a courtesy, I said: 'Excuse me. But isn't it customary in polite society to greet with gracious cheer?'

Even the birds sitting in the trees ceased their celebratory chants. You could hear a pin plop onto the fifteenth floor carpet. The Big Baas man stopped and regarded me. He raised his spectacles, like so, and considered his reply to Jabulani the watchman.

I am telling you now, I did not so much as blink when the Big Baas regarded me as he did. I was, I knew, in the right and so sat even more erect on my seat and buzzed in Madam Jane, who each morning, I observed, arrived no less than twenty-five minutes late for work for Mr Baas Brown. When Madam Jane saw the Big Baas she went pink and explained about the gridlock traffic and her misplaced house keys. Then she shook her umbrella and slunk up the stairs, not waiting for me to call the lift for her as usual. Without a word Big Baas produced from his right jacket pocket a small notebook. He opened it. He wrote down my name, spelling it, I could not help but notice, incorrectly. Then he snapped the notebook shut, slipped it and his gold pen back into his pocket, and smiled. I should have known then, it was the smile of a cat about to ambush a mouse.

Next morning I arrive at work. On time. I am never tardy. Not once in five and a half years can you make such a complaint about me. The manager of the building Baas de Klerk was waiting. Behind the desk there was another man sitting in my position, wearing a uniform identical to mine – the new watchman for the tower of Webber Steel Company. When he saw me, Mr de Klerk stood up straight. 'Pack up, Jabulani, Big Baas says you're out.' He pushed my last pay packet into my hands and seeing how my surprise rooted my feet to the ground, spat, 'Fok off, will you!'

Perhaps I should have kept quiet. Perhaps. But as I have already explained, I had spent too many years of my life already biting my tongue with these people. Besides, I had so many new words with which to express my emotions, in a language I knew this white man could for sure understand. I began. When I reached the word, 'conceited', the manager's normally pale face grew very red, right down to his blue shirt collar. He had the new man remove me from the premises. My black brother could not look at me, but in silence and moving very fast he followed the white man's orders and, taking me by the shirt scruff, threw me so I landed with great indignity amongst the crowds on the bustling morning promenade.

Fok man, this place really it is too dark. Even for the forgotten like us. So dark it makes me think maybe you are not really there and I am talking only to myself. Ha, I will not deny it. Sometimes on a night like this I long for a candle's watery light, but I must think of my neighbours. They would not like it – they have grown accustomed to this darkness and anyway the only lights allowed by the warders to burn at night are the security lamps beyond the steel door along the passages. This is what it is to be blind,

Jabulani. That is what I tell myself often. To be as blind as the whites.

You know, even in the daytime it is not dark like now but it is not light, which is why it's good to speak too. Somehow speaking helps, even to yourself. Makes you feel less alone. What else is good? Small, humble acts but they mean a lot. For example, every morning, first thing I do is I make the bed. I do not wait for my bedfellows David or Xela to take some initiative. Next, I pull my crate out from under the bed and count my possessions to make sure no bastard has tried to steal from me in the night. That crate cost me one rand. I acquired it from Hoppie the credit card thief. It is very useful, a most priceless asset. I use it for a table. And on my table I count: one tin opener, yebo; one roll of toilet paper, almost finished, yebo; two bars of Sunlight soap, one already thin, the other brand new still in its wax paper, yebo; one packet of cigarettes – last count with three left inside, yebo; one plastic comb with a broken tooth, the third from the right, yebo; a box of Lion matches – last count, five matches left inside. Yebo. Every morning I comb my hair and groom my beard.

Other complaints. The dirt. You know the smell of dirt? I do not mean a little bit of dust that lies next to the lift doors in the morning, I mean *real* dirt. Every morning the warders come and open the cells for the cleaning teams down the passage from cells 16 and 18. We hear them go. Talking, even joking. I recognise the same voices day after day but I do not know the bodies they belong to, the faces. I imagine fat, thin, tall, short, but for sure, all shades of brown. I imagine petty thieves, alcoholics, gamblers, petty brawlers. The cleaning men move as one on their hands and knees scrubbing and singing like kaffir slaves. We can hear their brushes scraping. Every day, at the end of the day, the cleaning teams go back into their cells. Clang click click, they are locked in again. They obey. Why fight when you know four months and you're out? You have a future to preserve, right? Anyway we have heard their brushes, or maybe just imagined them. Because this place – the staircases, eating mess, showers, passages, toilets, fok the toilets – they are just as fokking filthy as before.

I have a nose which is very sensitive to the smells of a place. So a game I play on a night like this when I cannot sleep is to try and pick out each smell one by one. Empty tin of sweet condensed milk. Dagga ash. These blankets. How many men have slept in these grey donkey blankets? And what has become of those men? They never wash these blankets, that's why the lice are always there. And our bodies? Once a week, forty men, one whole cell, in the shower at one time. One minute the water rushes down, pish pish, bounces off the white tiles and for a moment reminds you of falling rain. Scrub scrub, careful not to turn your back or you might regret it. Then the water stops. Still soap in your eyes. Voices come, loud, screaming: 'Prisoners! Prisoners Must Go Back To Cell 21!' No such word as 'please'. No towels. Back into old dirty clothes. Hurry hurry, others are waiting shivering down the passage. Feet still wet, so uncomfortable in your boots.

So what happened? The rest of the story. After I lost my job at Webber Steel Company I found it very hard to get work as a watchman. I wrote to Gabisile. I did not want her to worry, but I had to tell her the truth. Also I sent the last of my pay packet, my last seventy rands.

Eventually I did find work, but it was as a construction labourer. We men had a very inferior deal. Long hours, low wages, by the end of the day we were so tired we could hardly walk. But I still had that book, and each day after laying bricks and mixing concrete, transporting wheelbarrows of stone and rubble, my black brothers and I would sit together around a fire in an old petrol barrel, drinking beer and laughing at the words we found inside. I read it out loud so that even the men who could not read could also know. Big English words, words my black brothers might never have believed the white man actually possessed if I did not have the proof of it myself, in black and white, open on my lap. Decency, Humanity, Humility – we would sit around that book and how we laughed at our discoveries. That gave us extra power, I can tell you, laughing at what the white man could not remember. Thinking what word we would teach our Big Baas foreman next time he called us Boy. But inside, I am telling you now, we were crying; crying, yes, and very angry.

When the police picked me up and took me to the station, they first left in me in a very small cell, much much smaller than this one. It was so small you could not stand up, you could only crawl like an infant. I was all alone with only cardboard on the floor. That cell was very dark, darker even than this place and there were rats, rats as big as stray Soweto cats. They left me there for a few days. They did not tell me why I was arrested. I thought to myself all the time that I was sitting on that cardboard, there has been some mistake, some sort of white man's oversight. Then one morning they came to fetch me and took me to another room, bigger than the other room, a man could stand up. A very bright room with a chair in it. They tied me to the chair with my hands behind my back so that I could not move and pulled down my pants.

They said, 'You are Jacob Kameno.'

'No,' I said, 'I am Jabulani Ndlela.'

'Yes', they said, 'You are Jabulani Kameno, terrorist.' These whites and their fokking words, I thought to myself, nothing means as it should.

They said, 'You are a terrorist.'

I said, 'I am not a terrorist.'

They said, 'You are a terrorist and you are a Communist.'

I said, 'I am not a terrorist and I am not a Communist.'

They said, 'You are inciting people to commit violence.'

I said, 'I am not.' That was when they brought out the dictionary and held it in front of me. 'What are you using this for, kaffir? Hey? Choir practice? We know you have used this book to create terrorists.'

I said, 'No!' I said, ' I am simply teaching them about your language.'

'You have bitten the hand that feeds you.'

I looked at the two policemen's hands, now curled into fists ready to beat me. Their hands did not look bitten to me.

First, my friend, they beat me with that dictionary on my private parts. Then they made me eat the dictionary page by page. It is a very thick book, the number of pages I must tear and eat is eight hundred and sixty-four. It took me almost two days. They did not give me any water. In the end I had such cramps, I cried and could not walk. And those words, they are still inside me.

When they were beating me I said to them, 'How can you do this? This is your language!'

Then they took me to the magistrate's court. The magistrate took one look at me. I did not, I admit, look very good. My face was swollen from my many beatings. I had terrible shooting pains up my backside. The magistrate took one look and thought, here is a guilty man. He said, 'Terrorist! Life!' But really he meant 'Death'.

I wrote one last letter to my Gabisile. I said: 'Dearest wife, My effort to educate the white man has failed. I am going to prison. Life. No chance of parole. How are the children? How goes their work at school?'

My Gabisile wrote back saying: 'Look what you have done! Now the children and I will starve.'

I received no more letters from her for a year and a half. Then a letter: Gabisile was taking up with another man.

Try as hard as I do, I have learnt nothing can protect you from the difficult past forever. You know, I have not received one letter from my wife and my daughters – my Ntombikayise or Umzali, Zongile or Busiso. Now it is fourteen years I am here. Every three months when the post comes I cheat myself, just for the time it takes to distribute the envelopes from the first to the last. But Zola is more fortunate than I am. A few weeks ago he received a letter. It ripped open old wounds in me, thoughts and feelings so carefully pushed down, buried beneath all this thick concrete. It tells of how his son is getting married to a Zulu girl. You know who it is? My eldest, Ntombikayise.

So I decided: I would ask permission to go to the wedding. Me, a lifer. No chance, right? Not even on compassionate grounds. The other men did not even hesitate to tell me, no fokking chance of it. They told me about that Gada, in cell 10 – whole family killed in a fire, burnt to death: wife. seven babies, his parents, everybody. Not even him, not even for a funeral. Still I got it into my crazy head, I was going to write a letter, I might have a chance. Who can say not? The other men kept quiet.

Today I heard. Coetzee came to fetch me. We all stood with our hands up against the wall, backs to the warders as is expected.

'Prisoner 602/73 Kameno?'

'Yes, Sir.'

'Come!'

'Yes, Sir.'

He took me to the office. Then he gave me the letter from the Big Baas warder.

'Can you read, Kameno?'

'Yes, I can read.'

So they gave me a chance to read it for myself. 'Regret. Exceptions impossible.' Can you believe that my friend? All these years I have been here and still they have learnt fok all. They write 'Regret' but they mean 'No regret', they write 'Impossible' but they mean 'Do not want to'.

As soon as I walked in here, back into this place I am forced to call my only home, the other men saw from my expression, not good news. Very bad news. They kept clear. I admit I felt angry, so angry that I thought to myself, one of these days, Jabulani, they may succeed in making a kaffir out of you after all. A man who is not a man, a man who rages like a wild beast against the walls of this prison cage.

I went and sat on this bed and could not speak one word to anyone.

Eventually Xela came to talk with me. Very gently he said, 'That's why, Comrade Jabulani, there can only be one time for prisoners like us, the present. This is our life now. Try to forget the past. Also hopes, dreams, family. Push all of it from your mind. They took it away soon as they gave us Life. No hope of parole.'

But you know, still I cannot help it. I am in the dark, yes, I am in the dark with many and yet completely alone. No wife, no children, no future. But I must speak. I hope that somehow, somewhere across this wide silence you can hear me cry out.

THE MANGO TREE

The trouble began early, in pre-dawn darkness. Asleep, they were all asleep, their houses filled with snoring and dreams. Darkness, dreams and, with the last of the late-night shebeens finally closed, a fragile silence. Was that not their intention, Mathapelo has been wondering to herself these past two hours, to catch those amakwerekweres unawares? Still asleep in warm beds, suspecting nothing? Mathapelo circles her arms around her waist and begins to shiver.

This morning, two hours ago, at approximately half past five, Mathapelo had stood in her nightdress in her kitchen and listened to the sound of the men calling out from the darkness: 'Leave your houses, abandon your possessions, return to your own countries or prepare to die here!' She had stood and listened and heard, heard their singing and chanting. She had needed to use the toilet, that is why she was awake. But when she heard the men, heard their words, then she realised that serious trouble was coming and that if she stayed where she was, in her house so near to the homes of the foreigners, then she too would be in danger.

Mathapelo embraces herself harder. She runs her eyes along the cracks that decorate the plaster walls like thoughts until they reach the wooden crucifix that sits in the centre of the classroom wall, beside the poster explaining about HIV/Aids and another about how to wash hands correctly before preparing food. No, she is no saint. But would she nonetheless die like one today?, she wondered this morning, standing trembling in her dark kitchen, too terrified to light a lamp or even to move. She felt she could hardly breathe. Would she too be mistaken for a foreigner, like her neighbours, and be burnt alive? Would her house and humble possessions also be looted? Her growing sense of terror threatened to paralyse her.

Mathapelo steps forwards into the sun. She would like its faint, delicate beams to warm her bones, to take the bite off her inner chill, but it does not seem to possess the power to do so. Something warm, that is what she wishes for, even the sweatshirt her sister sent her as a gift for Christmas last year. Of course did not have the heart to tell her that by now she should know that she is not the sort of woman to wear such an item. What does her sister think, that she is one of her students? A soccer fan, Bafana Bafana, Banana Banana? It is all the same to her. It is like denims, jeans. She is proud that still she does not own any, she will die never having worn a pair. But even that bright yellow sweatshirt, too baggy, too long, she would be grateful for at this moment.

There was no time to think of such things this morning. She dressed as quickly as she could, putting on whatever was to hand, a skirt, a shirt, but she forgot her woollen cardigan as she fled into the streets, up the back alleys between the houses, taking the shortest route possible to this school after emptying her bladder in a drain. And yes, it is true, she did not think of her Congolese neighbours, even though she knows the wife of the young man is expecting a baby soon and just last month they lent her

some Omo when hers ran out. She did not think of them or
the other amakwerekweres, some of whom she does, it is
true, know by sight or even by name. She thought only of
herself. Yes, only of saving her own skin. But if she did not
do it, who would? Hey? Who?

Another involuntary shudder passes up and down
Mathapelo's spine. She turns away from the window to
look at the empty classroom benches. And the learners?
None. None have come. Mathapelo steps back to the
window. Punctuality or punishment, that is the school
motto, although few adhere to it – not the learners and not
the staff either. Will any students be so courageous, she
wonders, to attempt to come to study today or are terrified
parents keeping them all at home? Mathapelo looks at her
watch. Seven thirty-five. If some were going to come they
would almost certainly be here by now. So there can be no
doubt, just she and Mr Pata the school principal will be in
school today. At least she is not alone.

She saw Mr Pata arrive, what?, it cannot be more than
fifteen minutes ago. Saw how he parked his car in the staff
car park, watched as he locked the driver's door on that
dusty grassless field, walked to the school gate, unlocked
it, entered, and locked it again behind him. Then watched
as he crossed the courtyard, past the mango tree, and went
into his office. It is good not to be here alone, she had told
herself, even though she knows in her heart that Mr Pata
is as oblivious to her presence as he is to her terror. Still,
the sound of him now, typing in his office, the knowledge
that she is not entirely alone here at the school on a day
such a this, with those men, who are still too close, doing
what they are doing, is a comfort to her. The muffled yet
distinct hammer of typewriter keys, letter after rapid letter,
a comfort however false, however illusory. And yet part

of her cannot help but wonder how he can do it, just go on like that with ordinary school business as if nothing else is going on. Is he not afraid? She herself has tried to get on with odd jobs, this and that, writing the date and morning study task on the board for the learners, long division, but she cannot do it. Cannot concentrate. *How can he?*

Mathapelo's gaze moves nervously beyond the gates and down the school's short dirt driveway. Should she go to Mr Pata? No, he is no friend of hers, would offer her no real support, would consider her perhaps even foolish for being so afraid. Why would they come here to the school?, he would ask. It is the foreigners they're after and we're not harbouring any. Still, she prays that Mr Pata locked the school gate behind him securely. But if some pupils do arrive, will she then be forced to leave the safety of this classroom, of these high brick walls, to let them in?

In the distance it seems to her for a moment that two figures are indeed approaching. A trick of her imagination, for certain, because no student would come, not with the gangs of men moving through the settlement like packs of wild hyenas fighting over every morsel. Unless, unless the men themselves were coming to loot the school.

Two boys. Yes, they *are* real, they are real after all. But how? Where have they come from? Mathapelo leans forward into the window and the sun. Yes, yes, she blinks, she can see better, through the gates and just beyond. Something about these two who seem to have suddenly materialised out of thin air, in spite of the troubles up the road, something about them tells Mathapelo that she ought to stop and take proper notice: no school uniforms. Oh, but then… 'Oh!' Mathapelo, surprised, says the word out loud.

The sound of her own voice startles her. 'Oh my, but these two are amakwerekwere children!'

It is plain to her now, now that Mathapelo can see them clearly beside the fence. From their dark complexions, the shapes of their faces. Not local children. No, not at all. Foreigners, amakwerekwere. But why? Are they here because of the troubles? Are they at the school seeking sanctuary? What is Mathapelo to do?

Shame for them. Still what can she be expected to do, hey? Normally, she knows, it is her duty to discourage such foreign children who are not registered with the school from loitering around the school gates and potentially, as Mr Pata puts it, enticing the respectable local children of the primary school into bad habits. 'Even the youngest amakwerekwere child can possess its parents' criminal instincts. Their parents as we know, are like stray dogs taking what they can from our land.' And it is hard enough to teach our young students right from wrong, the headmaster warns, what with their own fathers drinking at Auntie Kishi's or gambling, throwing dice, and their mothers always working out of the house.

Yes, she should chase them away. Clearly they are not pupils from the school, they would be wearing school uniforms if they were and these two definitely are not, and might they not bring the troubles here to roost? Might they not put pupils who do come to study, if any do come, in jeopardy? Chase them away, scatter them back up the road. That would be the normal routine, unspoken school procedure: rules, normality, order. And yet, surely today with all that is going on, surely, she cannot help asking herself, can she actually bring herself to do it? Are they not, after all, only children?

Mathapelo is still considering what to do when she sees, to her surprise, the boys moving along the fence. When they come to the hole in the wire – the same one that Mathapelo has seen late children slip through in the past – they stop. Mathapelo holds her breath. Her eyes narrow as she watches the tallest boy squeeze through. She watches, her breath frozen painfully in her chest. She has seen enough children in her time, taught enough learners these past twenty-eight years, to be quite sure now, as she watches the first boy wriggle through, that he is not only the tallest of the pair, but also the eldest. It is he who goes first and holds the springing flap of barbed wire fence back for the smallest boy so that it does not tear at his face. Mathapelo observes these two barefoot boys as they hold hands, the taller, older boy leading the other, his brother; yes, she is sure now that they are brothers and from Nigeria or Congo, or some other West African backwater, just look at their colouring, black as burnt-out cooking pots, as the tar roads that carry them to our cities over the borders, thinks Mathapelo. She watches as they move cautiously across the playground courtyard, towards what? Where are they going? If they look as if they are going to break into one of the classrooms and attempt to steal a piece of school property, an already much too scarce textbook or chair or such like, she will not hesitate to sound the alarm. But they pass the Grade 3 and 4 rooms and edge closer to the playground's east side. To do what? What are these two up to? What sort of mischief, hey?

Oh, I see, Mathapelo says to herself. A plastic bag each. unmistakable yellow of Shoprite. Mathpelo watches as each boy draws one from his pocket. The mango tree, she should have guessed it. They have come to steal from the mango tree, imagine it! Maybe this is some sort of revenge for what

114

is happening, a revenge on their part, small but pointed, to break into the local primary school and help themselves to the fruit of the glorious mango tree – an act they certainly know to be forbidden, whilst all around them locals attack their houses and claim their possessions.

The mango tree that stands on the east side of the school courtyard is a particularly beautiful mango tree, the only mango tree, in fact, left directly inside the settlement (all the others were long ago chopped down, their wood used for other practical matters). It is a rare feature of the otherwise very ordinary-looking school. During her lunch hour or idle moments in the classroom while the children work in silence, Mathapelo likes to stand beside this window and watch the mango tree across the courtyard stir calmly in the breeze. Close your eyes for a moment when you pass it on a particularly windy day on your way to the staff room or if you are on playground duty and its leaves make the soothing, sweeping sounds of the women's long skirts in your home village, of tender lovers' sighs in the American romantic comedy films at the cinema in town.

Mathapelo opens her eyes. She straightens her blouse. Yes. Anyhow, it is a good tree, always green, healthy, alive, vibrant, a nice and necessary contrast to the otherwise bare red-dust courtyard where crowds of children line up for the head count, followed by one of Mr Pata's speeches and then the national anthem and a hymn each morning. Most years, these past six since Mathapelo first came to teach here at this school, it has borne fruit right through to the end of summer, from Christmas sometimes right through until the start of autumn – even sometimes as late as this month of April. It is loaded with fruit right now, its second or third but certainly final harvest. Normally the senior prefects collect the fruit in plastic buckets, for which they are each permitted a single delicious mango. The rest the teachers divide amongst themselves.

These boys – Congolese, no Zimbabwean (she thinks that actually they must be from Zim, they are not so dark after all, out of the shadows) – are still approaching the tree, yellow Shoprite bags ready. They have not seen Mathapelo yet. Normally if they knew that she, a teacher from the school, was watching, Mathapelo nods to herself, well, they would for sure not go near it. All the settlement children know. They know, indeed, for sure they do, amakwerekwere children or one of their own. They know, you do not dare take fruit from the mango tree of Pulla Primary School, because if you do you can be sure that there will be trouble. Mr Pata, he is going to find you whoever you are, wherever you live, and beat you black and blue with his bamboo cane. Mr Pata is very strict about it. Because the mangoes belong to the school he says, and local people yes, but first and foremost the school, and so any child caught with his or her face smeared sticky with yellow and hastily guzzled mango juice, has committed, in Mr Pata's eyes, a crime, yes, even a sin. These foreign boys, from whichever country they and their parents have come, they must either be very hungry or very foolish or very brave or all three to take such a risk. And on a day like today. With what is going on? Mathapelo swallows.

Again she remembers. Faces tearful, the houses, chaos and confusions just a few hours ago and still going on now. No, best not to dwell on it. What could she have done for them, brought them all with her to the school? Ridiculous. Her hands were tied. Nothing, she could do nothing, the gangs would have turned on her too; and she, just a woman, an ordinary woman, a teacher, with no capacity for such battles.

They have stopped at the foot of the tree, Shoprite bags ready. Mathapelo watches as the smaller boy wipes the snot from his nose on his sleeve and waits for the other boy, his brother, to hoist him into the lower branches. And all the while, their eyes on the headmaster's door. They do not need to look, Mathapelo thinks to herself. Just listen to that clacking of the typewriter, clackety clackety clack, like train wheels hurtling to an unknown destination. Yes, there they go, up and up, like jungle gorillas, like baboons. Why aren't their parents looking after them? Where are their parents now? Close by?

She sucks her teeth. She is sorry for them, sure. And guilty – yes, all right, she admits it. But what can she do? Just let them have the fruit today. Have it, take as much as you want and can put into your plastics bags. If she is being honest, she has always thought the headmaster too strict about this, not that she has ever dared tell him so. No, she has never dared. Many of the amakwerekwere children who attend classes, their parents newly arrived over the border, do come to school hungry and it would not have harmed the tree, she supposes, to give away some of the fruit to the very poorest. That Mozambican girl, Monica, with arms like bush sticks. But to tell Mr Pata that. Oh no, she can only imagine one of his rages or worse.

Not that she is condoning theft, of course she is not, and naturally she too is as concerned for the local children as their own mothers are, but what harm can it be to allow these two hungry boys – Mozambican, Zimbabwean, Congolese, whatever they are – a little fruit? To show some compassion? And on a bitter and ugly day like today. No, she will not go out and stop them. To hell with Mr Pata. She will remain here in this temporary sanctuary, safe from all the ugliness outside for a long as possible. Yes, let Joseph

Pata handle it if he thinks it so necessary. She has enough to worry about.

Mathapelo walks to her desk in the far corner of the classroom. She sits down behind it, facing the empty row of desks and benches, far too few for the number of pupils she is expected to teach. Almost forty boys and girls must be squeezed each day into this room, a room designed, she is sure, to hold no more than twenty-nine, perhaps thirty. The room smells faintly of dust even though she airs it regularly and her pupils must sweep it every day. A little bit damp too; the mould beneath the window smells of loamy soil and grows worse in the rainy season. The wooden furniture, it looks old and worn, which is what it is, the benches inherited from a church in Haenertsburg and used for goodness knows how many years by goodness knows how many pupils and congregants, and yet is far superior, in Mathapelo's opinion, to the cheap plastic chairs the government now supplies and which hardly seem to survive a year or two before they crack and cannot be mended. And there is something about it in the pale beams of early morning sunlight that makes the wood seem almost holy. The typewriter is, yes, it is still hammering, the office door still closed, the men still out in the streets, moving together in packs. How *can* Joseph Pata just go on working as though nothing terrible is going on? She cannot understand it. But she was a coward too this morning, yes, she knows it.

Across the window, a blue and brown bird darts past. And a flash of yellow: plastic. Mathapelo blinks. Yes, the two amakwerekwere boys are climbing, climbing, and picking for sure. But at least if she does not see them she cannot be accused of complicity. If she is confronted by Mr Pata she will claim only ignorance.

Mathapelo does not want to be unfair to Mr Pata. He is generally not such a terrible man, not so different from other headmasters she has known in her teaching career. But he does have a particularly potent distrust of foreigners. And yes, those foreign children who join the school, it cannot be denied, they have a worse time of it as far as he is concerned. There have been times, many over the past six years since she came to the school, that Mr Joseph Pata's actions, some of his policies and his treatment of the amakwerekwe pupils and their parents in particular, well, they have made her uneasy. The mango tree has already sprung to mind. But there is also the example of his Monday morning inspections. Mathapelo purses her lips and runs her tongue over her top teeth. Her tongue rests lightly in the gap between the front two. Yes, it is true. Those inspections can be bad and she does despise them as a consequence.

At the beginning of every week, as the children of her class settle down for the first lesson of the day, in her case, arithmetic, Joseph Pata arrives in Mathapelo's doorway with a sombre expression set on his broad, bearded face, like grave lines carved into potter's clay. During the ten-minute inspection that follows, Mathapelo has no choice but to stand impotently behind this very desk, her back to the coolness of the cracked chalkboard, her eyes on the window in the opposite wall, with its wire mesh, and wait for the headmaster to examine the forty pupils in her class. She can hardly bear it and each Monday must swallow her own indignity and wounded pride, sure, as well as her compassion for her young pupils, who certainly greet all of Mr Pata's visits with visible trepidation. Like an uncooked sweet potato, these emotions sit stuck in her throat as Joseph Pata sternly addresses her pupils. He examines fingernails and uniforms. Both boys and girls are expected to be clean and, in the case of their uniforms, not in too great a state of disrepair, or they receive a thrashing. What makes the whole situation truly unbearable, however, is the fact that – and no one present could deny this – Mr Pata appears to be far more critical, far less willing to compromise, when it comes to the three amakwerekwere pupils in her class. 'They know what is expected of them. This is South Africa! A civilised country, not their jungles.'

At the beginning of each term, the Monday morning agony is compounded by the list that Mr Pata possesses, a list of all the pupils who have not yet made the necessary contributions to their school fees. Once again it is the amakwerekwere pupils who suffer most. Those pupils are frequently sent home, their heads hung in shame, humiliation like the taste of raw sewage in their mouths. But Mr Pata is unapologetic. 'Without money our school cannot remain open. We cannot be expected to subsidise these foreigners. We are not a charity. If they want their children to attend the primary school, then they must pay like everyone else.'

Afterwards, Mathapelo knows, Joseph Pata returns to his office and sits behind his desk and typewriter, that very same typewriter that he prefers, he says, over any computer, that one which is clattering away right now and which is source of great pride for him in his otherwise bare principal's office, and types out identical suspension or reprimand slips for the offending foreign parents.

Mathapelo sighs. But they do not argue with Mr Pata. Not the parents, not the staff, not even she herself – and although she is, for sure, one of the teachers affected by the constant financial shortfalls caused by ungenerous government funding and those school fee evaders, as Mr Pata likes to call them, she does feel a certain sympathy each term for those who cannot pay, especially the amakwerewere parents, many of whom, she knows, find it difficult to find good jobs and have only recently arrived in the Polokwane settlement from their home countries; parents probably not so different from those of the two hungry little baboons stealing fruit right now, fresh over the border no doubt, smuggled in, one way or another.

But no, no one is willing to stick out their own necks to argue. No one has the courage. Perhaps they really believe what Mr Pata says about the questionable moral character of the foreigners they see arriving each day in the settlement. Perhaps they are even like those gangs of men out in the streets, blaming those same men for having no jobs or for crime and disease. Or perhaps they, like her, are simply afraid and cowards, afraid of jeopardising their jobs. Because she does love her job. Loves it in spite of everything – poor pay, overcrowding, not enough textbooks and the difficult knowledge that many of her learners sit through her class with empty bellies. Yes, sure. And what about Mr Pata? Him too. Still, she could imagine herself doing no other job, it is what she was born to do. She has known this fact since she was just a girl. So all the unpleasant compromises over the years, and there have been more and more as time has gone on, she has learnt to accept them. Not gladly, no, of course not, but with the hard realism and fatalism of one who knows that it is what must be done in order to survive.

There was a time in the school, it is true, a time many years ago when she first began here and when the situation with the foreigners first began to grow bad with more arriving in the settlement every day, that people stood up to Mr Pata. Sitting now in her deserted classroom, Mathapelo recalls one teacher who resigned soon after she arrived. John Mokena, yes, that was his name. Often he and Joseph Pata exchanged unpleasant words in the staffroom about what John Mokena saw as Mr Pata's distasteful and intolerable prejudices.

Why will Mr Pata not employ foreign teachers, when there is such a local shortage? 'Because it is against our policy. Local teachers first, local people first. And this is not only my policy. I have not pulled it from my hat, you know. It is the official government policy, Mr Mokena. I am certain I do not need to remind you of that.'

And the pupils? Why so strict with foreign pupils? Why so rigid when it comes to payment? Why so unwilling to offer any sort of credit?

A sigh from Mr Pata, as though he is talking to a particularly stupid student. Must he explain again and again when the answer is so clear? 'Do you want this school to gain the reputation of being a free ticket? We do not have to house these stray dogs no matter what, just because they come scratching at our door.' And then, perhaps sensing he had gone too far, 'I admire your Christian compassion, John, but this is not prejudice. It is a purely practical matter. You see, if those alien pupils, or any pupils for that matter, do not pay their fees, fail to comply with school rules, than how I am to be expected to pay you and all my other teaching staff? We would have no choice but to close, so you see I have the community's greater interests in mind. Also, with our proximity to the borders, I do not have to tell you how quickly news would spread of our being a soft touch. So, if the alien children must be sacrificed to safeguard the future of our own community, so be it. Let them go back to their own countries, let their alien governments pay for them.'

In spite of everything, Mathapelo smiles. 'Alien'. At first when she heard it, she thought, From what? And as for 'amakwerekwere', as for that – well, her own language, it never ceases to amaze her. It is because they say the foreigners cannot speak Xhosa, or Zulu, et cetera et cetera. Even their English sounds like the noisy rubbish of wild animals, that is what they say. They speak a big lot of *kwe kwe kwe*, like birds or monkeys in the trees at night. But, you know, in her experience that is not true. There are those who can speak South African languages and who do learn quickly. Their children, *they* do.

Mathapelo stands up. She regards her empty classroom. No, there is no use in denying it, no running from it or trying to hide from it any longer. 'We have all been great fools,' she says to the ghost of John Mokena, 'I just as much as the others. Perhaps if we had joined you, perhaps if we had tried to make a plan to bring all the people together. But we were afraid, and now look, everything here around us has started to fall apart.' Mathapelo walks to the chalkboard. She wants to do *something*, anything, but what?

Suddenly there is shouting, and Mathapelo's head snaps up. It's Mr Pata! Mathapelo hurries to the window. The headmaster's door stands wide open and she can see him marching across the courtyard towards the mango tree. Mathapelo steps right up to the window. She presses her nose against the rusty wire so that she can see him clearly. He is yelling as he strides forwards, his bearded face outraged and explosive, his voice booming against the prefabricated buildings and zinc rooftops, 'That's not your tree! Get down this instant! You filthy thieves! I will murder

123

you with my own hands!' Above his head he is swinging the long punishment bamboo.

Mathapelo searches for the two brothers. They were in the mango tree just a few minutes ago. She has almost forgotten about them. Are they still there? Yes, holding the fruit hungrily to their lips. Plastic bags? Full. She grits her teeth. Her belly aches. So, caught red-handed; today, of all days, they will be beaten to within an inch of their lives by Mr Pata, she is sure of it.

But the boys are not moving. Without knowing how it happens, Mathapelo finds herself outside. She must have run. The astonished Mr Pata is looking at her, his mouth opening and closing in surprise like a fish pulled fresh from the river. No sound comes out from that mouth. The boys, they too are looking at her too without speaking a word.

When Mr Pata speaks, Mathapelo can read the fury on his face. He speaks through gritted teeth. See how he trembles in his anger, thinks Mathapelo. 'Mrs Mhlabeni, what are you doing? Get out of my way, you stupid woman, or I will make you.'

But Mathapelo shakes her head. No, she will not move.

'Mrs Mhlabeni, I ask you one last time…'

No. Mathapelo squares her shoulders and looks at Mr Pata, right in his eyes. She is ready, ready for any blow he may choose to administer or devise, but she will not move. No, she says, 'No.'

But this place is my home

Monday, six thirty in the morning, and Michael Ntandazo is squatting on the grass at the side of the N2 motorway a few feet from the Nyanga boundary fence. From his seat on the ground Michael can observe, on one hand, the motorway leading to the city and all its rushing traffic and, on the other, the township itself as it gradually shakes off the weekend's excesses. Beyond the fence, windows are already illuminated and shack doors propped open with bricks. Soon, Michael knows, yawning men and women will appear and like sleepwalkers make their way through the dim streets to the taxi-bus terminals where they will catch lifts to the city centre or their madams' kitchens in the suburbs. Another Monday morning, thinks Michael, *kak* as it always is with the whole miserable week unrolling before you like so many days of torture. But not for him. No. For him this Monday is worse than *kak*. Much much worse. For him this Monday is like being in *hell*.

Ja ja ja. Wearily Michael scratches at the stubble on his chin and presses his bare feet into the tattered grass. A pair of stray dogs search for rubbish scraps as yet another car hurtles past blindly. Michael sighs. During the night it was mostly lorries. But now that it is morning and the airplanes are arriving at the airport just over the near horizon, it is the tourists' motorcars, he is certain, that are tearing their way towards the Mother City.

He wants to stand up and tell them a thing or two. Give them a piece of what has been burning in this brain of his all night long as he sat shivering on this spot. Ha! Slowly Michael pushes himself up on to his cramped feet. He lets the woollen blanket Gugu gave him last night slip from his shoulders and fall to the ground as he, tugging up the waist of his sagging pyjama bottoms, staggers to the roadside.

He stands close, so close to the edge of the road that he can feel the cool roaring rush of the passing cars. One driver hoots. Another swerves. Good, thinks Michael, for sure these bastards can see him. Stretching out both of his thin brown arms at his sides, like Jesus Christ Himself sacrificed on the Cross, he shouts: 'You want to look, look! This is a black man, you bloody bastards.' With his right index finger he jabs in the direction of the township, the place nine hundred metres in, beyond the rusted corrugated iron rooftops, where the smoke is still rising, purple like a scar, 'And look! That's what you have done to my house!' Michael swallows hard. His throat is parched. It is because of last night's swallowed smoke and because he is exhausted.

Michael spits and slumps back on to the ground, his back turned deliberately on the oncoming motorway traffic. He picks up the donkey blanket, dusts it off and wraps it round his body, covering his head with it too. They will think that he is drunk, he knows it, another one who cannot hold his weekend beer. So what, let them think it.

Michael sniffs. He can still smell the stink of the fire coming from his skin and his clothes; yes, they are smeared with white ash, he knows. But where else? He sniffs, he smells. This blanket Gugu gave him? This also? Ja. Somehow last night the whole lot was contaminated. Michael kicks off the blanket. He would rather die of cold. He is about to throw it into the road under the wheels of a speeding car, when above his head he catches sight of a black bird dancing on the boundary fence that separates the township from the tar motorway and grassy bank. He remembers how, as a boy, he used to watch the hunting hawks circle on warm currents over the mealie fields of his village, swooping down to snatch a snake or a mouse. This bird before him now is different. A city bird, it twitches nervously from side to side, its small body silhouetted against the browns of the skew pondokke nearby. Looking for food, thinks Michael. His stomach groans. He is beginning to grow hungry too.

'So, probably you are wondering', says Michael, addressing the balancing bird, 'what I am doing sitting at the side of the motorway like this? Am I right? A man *my* age. A respectable man. Ha. Dressed like this.' Michael gestures down to his pyjama bottoms and his white short-sleeved sleeping vest streaked with soot, the blanket now crumpled at his bare feet, 'Practically naked. Ha! Good question. I'll tell you.' He leans forward and hisses, 'Tourists, those fokken bastards! And I am no bloody elephant, understand? No animal like you, hey hey. They want to look, they must go look someplace else. Khayelitsha. That's right. Soweto. Gugulethu right next door. Or stay in their own bloody countries.' Michael spins round to face the oncoming traffic again. 'You got it?! We do not want you!' He gestures irritably at the cars that continue to pass, his right fist raised in the air. 'Voetsak, man! Voetsak!' The bird has fled but the cars are relentless. They cannot be stopped and so the tourists too cannot be stopped. It is only a matter of time before they come to Nyanga and the Nvaba brothers get their wish. Agh, what does he care?, Michael thinks. He cares for nothing any more. Everything he cared for is gone. First her, his wife Yola, now their house. Let them come. Let the bloody tourists just come and take whatever is left.

The sorts of peoples who fly in airplanes, who now shoot down the motorway towards the city with no regard for him, had no interest in Nyanga as a tourist destination until just a few months ago. Michael remembers how it used to be. And he remembers the evening it all changed, though he could not have known at the time what troubles for him personally would soon follow.

It was January – now it is the beginning of April. Over free bottles of Red Label beer and homebrew, free Coke cooldrink for everybody, he sat with the others at the 8-foot-long tables of the Nvabas and listened to the Nvaba brothers laying down their plans and their goal: NYANGA. PUTTING IT ON THE TOURIST'S MAP IN TIME FOR WORLD CUP 2010. 'You know,' Vusi Nvaba said, leaning his big body, like a heavyweight boxer's body – like Mike Tyson's before he went soft in his head – across a trestle table, 'there is competition. In Jo'burg, Soweto. It possesses all that political history. And here in the Cape, next door Langa, and Gugulethu, and just down the N2, towards the coast, the famous Khayelitsha. Already that township has had two hit films made about it. Beach sand paves their streets. We have got to make this place more appealing to those same foreign tourists if we too are to profit from the riches of the World Cup. But we are close to the airport – that is our great asset.

There was a respectful silence as the brothers spoke. The Nvaba brothers are, after all, a powerful pair in Nyanga, important members of the council who decide so much of township business. Also, they control several important and growing enterprises, the most successful of which is their drinking tavern Nvaba's, which through a process of both clever promotion and intimidation the brothers have ensured is the most lucrative of its kind in Nyanga. The tourists were to be the brothers' most ambitious and potentially most lucrative venture yet.

But it would not be a simple task, said the brothers. The problem was, of course, safety. This, Mbhazima Nvaba, of more slender build than his brother and considered the real brains, always, of the Nvaba operations, explained to the assembled group of approximately two hundred residents and other carefully chosen guests. Or rather, he added, how to ensure the tourist felt safe. The second problem was the question of beauty, as the tourists who came would not want a real taste of township life. Not a case of the runs, not the smell of piss and shit that ran from the squatters' outhouse toilets with inadequate sewage and drainage systems. What they wanted was colour, local life, the darker hues of the Rainbow Nation, but not to have their senses offended by the sour smells and ungainly sights of *true* poverty and deprivation. Mbhazima smiled behind his Ray Ban sunglasses. Both brothers wore these, even inside, even, *my God*, thinks Michael, sometimes at night. It is a mark of their superior financial and social status. Michael does not like it. He has never liked it, and also how they always speak using large, complicated words as though they want to trick you. They are arrogant, it is true, always looking down on others, even their elders, though Michael did not realise it so much at the time. Now several weeks after the event, Michael shifts in irritation on the grass as he recalls.

Mbhazima spoke without standing up. 'Brothers and sisters, this is what those foreigners think of us. First, that we love to dance. You name it – time or place – we, like our President, can't stop our bodies and ourselves from moving. So, we must dance for our tourists in full tribal costume. The stuff we almost never put on now, we must dust it off and put it on.' Mbhazima paused only to take a sip of tea. 'Second, we love to sing. So, same as before. We will do it. Third, we are very industrious people. Tourists think they know how the African loves to recycle old rubbish, also because we are so poor. Not like those rich white bastards out at Clifton; we can work magic with what they throw away.' The younger brother held up his tin cup, once a green Cream Soda can, in demonstration. 'Fourth, we love to eat some really exotic foods – goat, buck. Fifth, we always smile as easily as children.' At this point Mbhazima broke into a very wide and handsome smile, which he held for a few seconds, like a man who was having his photograph taken. Then the smile vanished. 'Sixth, we love tradition and our heritage.'

The necessity was simple, Mbhazima continued: give the tourists what they wanted, what they expected. 'Show them a good time. And make them feel they are doing some really good charity by coming here, that their consciences can then be clear when afterwards they go and spend thousands of rands at the Waterfront shopping mall or on drinking their expensive wines.'

From his seat on a bench in the packed room, Michael listened. He did not utter his opinion during that first half hour. No one possessed the courage to interrupt these intelligent brothers and give their opinion. The Nvabas had considered all the necessary details, they said, and explained them all. First, the main entrance, where the tourists would inevitably pass through, would have to be neatened up, with all rubbish removed and a welcoming sign hung in plain view. It would be painted red, yellow, black, blue, green, white, all the colours of the nation's flag. That sign is already up and if Michael turns and strains his neck he can just make it out, hanging further down the motorway a little deeper into the township. Next, the shebeen itself would have to be redecorated. At the moment it was a bare place, without much (Vusi Nvaba smacked his lips) 'real African character'. Vusi paused for a moment and gulped from his glass of 7 Up. Michael watched with a certain amount of wonder as all the tiny bubbles dancing in Vusi's glass disappeared into the brother's large mouth. There was a murmur of approval from the assembled audience as they digested his words. The lids of oil drums would be collected and nailed to the walls, some animal skins found. Everything in the shebeen, it would be clear, would have come from somewhere and given a new life, like the new South Africa. A photograph of ex-President Nelson Mandela would have to be found too, and hung up in the entrance like a welcoming beacon, a stamp of benediction and approval.

There was discussion, also, of the menu. Michael's mouth had watered listening. Remembered now, it begins to again. Beer, mieliepap, Cokes, Fantas, chicken, goat. The menu would be printed in the eleven official languages and the sangoma brought in to do ritual exorcisms upon request…

Michael sighs deeply. His wife, his Yola, she was from a family of traditional healers. It is true; Christian or not, if

131

she said, 'You are going to die', then I am very sorry, you died. She could see, before things happened or after the event, why they had happened, good and bad. Once in church after the service she went and told a man, 'I am sorry to have to tell you this, my brother, but someone has put a curse on your family.' The man was not a local. He was a Zulu from Durban.

She said, 'I can tell you where the muti is. It is in a tin. When you killed an ox, someone took some blood. The tin is in a dark place, maybe in a cupboard or under a bed.'

She was, of course, absolutely right. For four years the man's close family had been dying out, two at a time. Very mysterious, no one knew why. The man returned to Durban and told his father everything. They wanted Yola to make the journey and meet with them. They telephoned her. How did she know all of this? Yola only shrugged. It was in her blood. But it turned out, that was not all that was in her blood. Cancer swam through her veins too, waiting for the moment when it could bear its deadly fruit. She knew that also, he is sure, but she did not want to upset him by telling him until it was too late.

If Yola were alive, this would not have happened. She would have known what to do. God. Michael leans forward and examines the grass. The patch where he is sitting is worn through by what?, dogs' bitter-smelling piss? How much he misses her.

Michael watches as, above the township fence, another bird on a cable wire momentarily loses its balance, then corrects itself and stays put. From the direction of the settlement a cock crows and further away, in some distant cradle of the town, street dogs bark together.

No. He shakes his head, he does not need to snoop or pay to know what is happening across the settlement inside those wood and steel shacks and the more wealthy and fortunate people's government brick home stands, right now, at this hour. This is his home and he knows, he knows for sure, that if there are women about, decent women like her, they will be up, already washed and dressed, now bent over their stoves preparing breakfast for their families. Agh. He cannot help it, he remembers, yes, he remembers how it once was. Michael squints at the sky above the houses. The familiar crash of shapes and colours. Their home for twenty-eight years, this place. Last stop, they always agreed, in what had proved a long and hard homeless journey from farm to farm. Always other people's, never his own *plek*, understand, until here. He knows it, he knows like this – Michael holds his weathered palm up into the gathering sunlight and shows it to a red car bulleting past along the motorway – like the streets and hills on his own palm. That is right. *He* is no tourist. No tourists here, only true citizens!

Bloody bastards, he wants those bloody foreigners in those bloody cars to know something more. The Nvaba brothers too. He is no *drol*. Normally at this time he would still be in his house, his own home built with his own two hands, not on the side of the street like this, like a piece of rubbish or a township dog's turd. He would have washed and shaved in the kitchen, in the steel basin. He would be dressed nicely and warmly by now, maybe because the air is a little chilly, wearing that red woollen jersey Yola knitted for him the winter before she died, and listening to the radio whilst having his breakfast. He does not mind the news but prefers music, maybe something like a woman singing with a good voice. He is a Christian man, he likes good Christian music about Jesus. Also hot coffee cooled and sweetened with creamy condensed milk from a tin, that is what he likes. The tins all kept in the cupboard that used to be beside the stove, kept exactly how she kept them. The fire probably finished them all off too. Maybe some stiff mieliepap sprinkled with three tablespoons of white sugar; he has a sweet tooth, that is true. His wife, she always said this. She put it in, she stirred it, she gave it to him. Michael closes his eyes and reaches forwards to takes the hot bowl of delicious heavy pap. His mouth is awash with saliva, his stomach almost nauseous now with hunger. But no, no chance – all gone. Michael opens his eyes and looks in the direction of the settlement. The smoke is still rising.

Those two boys, those two brothers, are very clever. He understands that now. First in that meeting they made everyone very excited, even him. Painted for them each a beautiful picture of how much good would come to the township with these foreign football tourists. How everyone would benefit, how nobody could lose. The government might even, the brothers said, be forced to make extra improvements. Then they said: 'But there is a problem.'

A problem! Oh no! The people's and the council members' hearts sank. Already they had spent the rands that these famous tourists had not yet pushed into their pockets. Already they had bought cars, televisions, cements to repair walls, fashions, wardrobes to hang them in. 'What thing? What thing?' they cried.

The brothers raised their hands for silence. Then they explained. The shebeen would have to be extended in order to accommodate the large groups of curious and respectful foreign faces. Now there was some mutterings

134

amongst those in the shebeen. The neighbourhood people were concerned. Extended how? How could it be? All that particular section of the township was packed. Around the shebeen, three family houses, including Michael's, and their backyard pondokke. What to do about those houses and the families who lived in them? Michael leant forward. This was him they were now talking about, him directly. Mbhazima took over again. Again that smile, slippery, Michael thought, slippery as Sunshine margarine smeared on the floor. Naturally those families would have to be relocated. For which there would be generous compensation.

Haai! Finally the audience, who until this moment, Michael thinks, were bewitched, came to life. *No!* Sitting here on the ground, weeks later, Michael feels the old stabbing surprise and shock. The houses around the shebeen? Those houses? Michael waited to hear. A muttering amongst the brothers and their helpers. Yes *those* houses, *those* families would have to be rehoused, repatriated, to another less crowded street, just around the corner.

More mutterings.

'Brothers and sisters, all Nyanga will benefit from the arrival of our new foreign guests. Think, brothers and sisters, think of the profits for all concerned.' Mbhazima said he was sure that if the people thought it through properly, then the temporary discomforts of the so few would not be allowed to stand in the way of prosperity for so many.

Money money money. That was all anyone seemed to talk about these days. What did Michael care? He had never possessed much of it and he did not expect it to come his way now, during the gathering twilight of his life. No.

His house could not be bought. The home where he had raised his five children and seen his wife pass away into the grave could not be given a price. It was beyond price, you understand.

An empty plastic Checkers bag has been blowing along the grass to where he sits. It flutters, caught on a twig at his feet. Michael looks at it but does not touch it.

In the sheeben, Michael took a deep breath, got to his feet and interrupted the brothers. 'What if we do not want to move?'

The room fell silent. All eyes were on Michael and the brothers to see what they would say to this challenge. Both brothers turned to look at Michael, their faces fixed in expressions of polite surprise. Then Vusi said, his smile and hands spread wide, like a politician's, 'Why would you want to stay, old man? The houses around here are some of the most ragged in the settlement. And you will be paid handsomely once the profits start.'

Michael shook his head and folded his arms. He would teach these two kids a lesson, something of the old ways, of respect for your elders, elders who have *lived*. He shook his index finger at them as he spoke. 'I have known you and your brother a long time, Vusi, since you were kids, since our families lived side by side in this street. You visited my sons and my daughters in my house. And my wife died in that house. Don't pretend you do not know it.' Michael turned to address the whole room, the faces of his friends and neighbours and the expressionless faces of the council members. 'My house cannot be bought. Understand that it has no price.' Michael sat down again and the room was completely silent. No one else dared stand up to support him.

Michael could see from Mbhazima's frown that he was greatly displeased, but he had more self-control than his older brother and a reputation for being of a milder temperament. 'Everything has a price, Tata,' he said finally.

Michael shook his head. Even now, sitting at the side of the motorway, he shakes it. No, not his house. The people in the cars shooting up and down this motorway need to understand. The Nvaba brothers too. Not his house.

'Enough talking, Mbhazima,' Vusi snapped, interrupting his younger brother, his smile now gone. He spoke only in English, 'You'll have one month to be out, old man.' Vusi's expression was hard like a brick. He jabbed a finger in Michael's direction and then at the rest of the audience to show he really meant business. 'The first tourist buses have been booked for three months' time, practice for all the soccer fans. This gives just enough time to make the necessary changes to the shebeen. You and the others families must go!'

The meeting was over. The council members shook the brothers' hands and retreated into their office. Other peoples gradually dispersed and Michael found himself sitting alone on the bench in the empty shebeen. They would not take his house. No no no.

Michael knew his house was not grand, but he was proud of certain features which he had given a great deal of thought to. For example, a door buzzer. Now it is true, it did not actually work, but it added a fine touch to the house to have one. To avoid confusion for callers and visitors, Michael had painted a notice on the door, one he had copied from a shop in town: 'Doorbell out of order. Please knock.' He had also built the house itself and repaired and improved it many times, and it had never, unlike many of the others, been washed away by the heavy Cape rains when the settlement was still unpaved. But it was not these home improvements or vanity on his part that mattered. What mattered most was, as he explained to the brothers, it was not just a house but a home of many memories and an important ghost – the ghost of his beloved wife Yola.

Still he saw her, early in the morning in particular, or late at night. A shadow passing by the window. A pleasant feeling in the air, or sometimes just the smell of her, when he cooked his samp over the two-point burner, or especially when he stirred the pap at the stove. When he stirred he saw her, stirring too. Every morning, except Sundays, six o'clock, her standing over the stove turning the pot of steaming breakfast pap with the wooden spoon. His Yola's fleshy arms, and round, solid body from behind, before she grew thin from the disease, how they moved with a soothing rhythm as she scooped and swirled the white, bubbling maize porridge until it was cooked stiff – just how he liked it. If you know someone intimately you know how their body moves when they perform certain actions. Each body has its own particular rhythm when it runs, when it walks, when it dances. She and her rhythm were everywhere in that house, from the curtains she had sewed from old fabric the farmer's wife no longer wanted and that she had brought with her to the city in 1986, to the kitchen table which bore the burn marks of plates that were too hot (Nolwazi, their youngest and most foolish daughter – God, that girl did not understand heat. How angry her mother was with her). He saw, he sees, he sees it all still in here – Michael touches his right temple – the house that still exists in his head even if in reality it is now no more than ash.

Fire. Michael knows very well from the car factory what fire does to metal, how it twists and makes it writhe. And plastic, how it melts and blisters like living skin. And paper! He should never have insulated the house with it. Cardboard, newspaper, adverts from magazines, and wood, how it burns easily, after its initial resistance. The bed, the three chairs, the kitchen table, all wood, all made with his own hands or bought by Yola with her hard-earned domestic's wages – to make things more beautiful, understand? To add her woman's touch. He should never... Each burns in its own time but it burns, it burns good. Each with its own smell but mixed together all only one thing, bitter rolling smoke thick enough to make a man choke.

After some initial protests, all the other neighbours bent to the Nvaba brothers' demands. Michael said No. Then four men had come to his home just two weeks ago and banged with their heavy fists on his door. Who bangs like that? thought Michael, putting down his coffee cup. In his life Michael had known only the police to bang like that.

'The Brothers Nvaba want to see you.'

The four men marched Michael to the shebeen office next door, where Mbhazima Nvaba was waiting for him. Mbhazima was in a good mood when Michael arrived. He greeted him warmly at the door, shaking Michael's hand in both of his and apologising for the inconvenience but explaining that he wanted to speak with Michael while his brother was out for the day. Then he gestured for the men outside to go away and leave them alone. 'But first bring me a cooldrink. You want something, Babu Michael?'

So, this one has not lost all of his upbringing, thought Michael. He still remembered something of how to treat his elders with respect. Michael stood up straighter and raised his head a little higher. 'Why not. A cooldrink. Thank you.'

'Coke?'

Michael nodded.

'Voted South Africa's favourite brand. My brother and I are planning on doing one of those business courses the government is now offering for young African men like ourselves. But that is another matter. Please sit down.'

Michael sat in the chair opposite Mbhazima's at the brother's desk. A man brought two Cokes and two glasses. Mbhazima poured his and waited until the door to the office was closed before starting to speak.

'I'm glad you came, Babu Michael. I understand you still have some reservations about our plans to put our little township on the map and I wanted to talk to you about them myself.'

'You can do as you wish to the township Mbhazima, only do not do it to my house.'

Mbhazima drank from the glass. Michael saw how he did not gulp at his drink as his older brother did, who, even as a child, Michael recalled, when they came to the house to eat, did not take time to savour his wife's cooking. When Mbhazima put the glass down, he leant back in his chair and sighed. 'With all due respect, Babu Michael, there is a bigger picture here than just your house or even this shebeen. People in this place need money. They need jobs. The young people. There is crime. You know how it is. These foreigners, these tourists will provide jobs and money.'

Michael nodded. 'I do not want to deprive anyone, but you know, it was the place where she, where my wife died. It was in that place that I laid her on the ground ready for burial.'

Mbhazima said nothing but Michael knew he was listening.

'So you see, I cannot.'

Mbhazima bent forwards and put his hands together on the table. Michael could see himself reflected in his sunglasses and could not help but notice that Mbhazima was wearing a large gold watch. He seemed to be considering something, 'And if I was to offer you money. More than the others?'

Michael looked down and shook his head. There was silence between the two men for a moment. Mbhazima sucked his lips together. Then he sighed a heavy sigh. 'Well, this is very disappointing to me, I will not deny that. I brought you here against my brother's wishes because of the long history our families have together.'

'Thank you, Mbhazima. I am pleased you have not forgotten our past together.'

'Just go home and sleep on it.'

Michael shook his head. 'But I tell you, I do not need to sleep on it. My mind is made up.'

Mbhazima nodded. 'I know what you have said. Just sleep on it. That's all I ask.'

Michael shrugged. The Nvaba boy opened the door for him, they shook hands and Michael left.

The following day he let them know his decision was still No. He heard nothing, no reply, but he was not worried. He and Mbhazima had parted on good terms, he was certain of it. But his neighbours, they were not so convinced. 'You know, everyone knows you do not make trouble with those two brothers. Everyone knows, you do not bother, it is not worth the sorrow,' his wife's old friend Gugu and other concerned neighbours told him when they came to see Michael and to warn him of the rumours. Stories of men found face down, bullet in the skull, their blood being slowly mopped up by the ground like gravy because it is said that they offended the brothers in some way or other. Of lives going up in clouds of smoke. The brothers were not tolerating any resistance to their plans to bring the foreign tourists to their shebeen. Why would they tolerate disagreement from him?, one neighbour asked Michael.

Agh, you know, Michael told that man, they are not so bad. When you have known a man as a kid, playing soccer with your own sons, dribbling and weaving on the street, it is different. Those boys came and ate in this very house, Yola cooked for them. They acknowledge the family relationship, he is sure that all would be well. But more than that, they were abakhwethas together, his eldest son Phumeza and that eldest Nvaba boy Vusi, in the same school they were initiated as men of the tribe. Together they set fire to their cardboard shelter. Wearing only white blankets and carrying their scorched iminqayi they walked away from their handiwork, and so it was that they saw the end of their childhoods together and greeted the beginning of adult responsibilities. So you see, he told Gugu and Busi, who both came to the house to try to convince him to reconsider, Vusi and his Phumeza are brothers.

Now, sitting on the grass, Michael laughs bitterly to himself. Ha! He had known their parents too, good people though dead for more than eight years. The place which is now the shebeen was once the spaza shop run by their mother. Yola would go there if she had not had time to stop at the supermarket on the way back from the home of the Barrys where she worked, though she resented the higher prices. And together both women sat on the Women-Only Club committee, organising necessary actions for the women of the township or acts of charity.

'Everything has changed since those days, Michael,' Gugu warned. 'This soccer money clouds everyone's brains worse than beer or dagga. The young no longer respect the old as they once did. Please, Michael, please be careful.'

He was asleep and dreaming when they struck. Bottles of lit petrol, no doubt the bottle leftovers from a weekend of profitable sales at 'Nvaba's'. One Molotov cocktail smashed through the kitchen window, the second, the one that woke him, through the window in the bedroom. A blazing meteorite in the dark room, it landed with a loud crash, then rolled, coming to rest at the chair on which he had hung his coat, not three feet from the foot of Michael's bed. The kitchen was already on fire. Within moments bright yellow and orange flames were licking up everything in their path in the bedroom too. Soon the coat, the papered walls and cheap wooden furniture were aflame – the blue curtains with green flowers on them that his wife had made. The air rolled with angry black smoke. Michael leapt from the bed; moving like a man thirty years younger, he made it out just in time through the blazing doorway, just before the wooden beams buckled in the heat bringing the wood walls down too, like flaming flimsy cardboard. The fire was so quick and so hungry that the neighbours could not help.

On his knees, coughing, spluttering, with stinging smoke tears streaming down his cheeks and onto his night vest, he watched as useless attempts were made. A group of about ten, using plastic buckets of water and dry earth, managed to put the flames out before the fire spread to other houses or the shebeen, that has already doubled in size. But for him it was too late. Long before dawn this morning, his house was completely gone. Finished and *klaar*. Stolen.

A taxi-bus ferrying the early departing township workers to the city centre and suburbs passes Michael on the roadside, its driver pressing on the horn to attract more customers. Michael is very hungry. Soon he will have to find a neighbour. He is certain Gugu or someone else will take him in for a few days until he can start again. Ha, he has started again so many times, he thinks he should be called the Start Again Man. What do you think, rock?, he asks a stone trodden down into the earth. And you, plastic bag? And you, birds? What about you, ugly motorcars? Michael talks into the invisible wind. He closes his eyes and listens. He leans forwards and listens, but the only sound is the busy road.

Other Modjaji Titles

Whiplash
by Tracey Farren

Invisible Earthquake
A Women's Journal Through Stillbirth
by Malika Ndlovu

Hester se Brood
Hester van der Walt

Undisciplined Heart
by Jane Katjavivi

The Thin Line
by Arja Salafranca

http://modjaji.book.co.za